ARIS AND PHILLIPS HISPANIC CLASSICS

T0313452

ANTÓNIO PEDRO

JUST A STORY
(Apenas uma narrativa)

Edited and with Introductory Articles by

Cláudia Pazos Alonso and Bruno Silva Rodrigues

Translated by

Mariana Gray de Castro

Aris & Phillips is an imprint of Oxbow Books

Published in the United Kingdom in 2015 by
OXBOW BOOKS
10 Hythe Bridge Street, Oxford OX1 2EW

and in the United States by
OXBOW BOOKS
908 Darby Road, Havertown, PA 19083

Hardback Edition: ISBN 978-1-91057-205-4
Paperback Edition: ISBN 978-1-91057-206-1

A CIP record for this book is available from the British Library

For a complete list of Aris & Phillips titles, please contact:

UNITED KINGDOM	UNITED STATES OF AMERICA
Oxbow Books	Oxbow Books
Telephone (01865) 241249	Telephone (800) 791-9354
Fax (01865) 794449	Fax (610) 853-9146
Email: oxbow@oxbowbooks.com	Email: queries@casemateacademic.com
www.oxbowbooks.com	www.casemateacademic.com/oxbow

Oxbow Books is part of the Casemate group

Front cover: Reproduction of the cover image designed by António Pedro for the first edition of *Apenas uma narrativa* (1942) © José-Augusto França

Printed and bound by CPI Group (UK) Ltd, Croydon, CR0 4YY

CONTENTS

ANTÓNIO PEDRO

António Pedro was exempted from military service on the grounds of excessive height. This could well be a metaphor for his life. He did not fit into any established mould and spent his life seeking something he could fit into, trying out various aesthetic experimentalisms current in his time and never settling in any of them. Nor did he ever settle for an exclusive practice of one of the arts at the expense of the others, regarding them all as complementary external forms of expressing the latent internal workings of the human mind. He was a poet and painter, and dedicated the last years of his life to the theatre. In Surrealism he found a way of giving conscious expression to the subconscious and, in Dimensionism, a fusion of words and visual images. In the theatre he found the expression of the fixed in the changeable – or the permanent in the transitory – through the transformation of the potential in a text into its living, ephemeral representation. In the words he used in *Pequeno Tratado de Encenação* (*A Short Treatise on Staging*): 'The art of staging' consists of 'making the word flesh' since 'the written word, on its own, does not exist'. He may have meant something similar when he wrote: 'there is no such thing as modern or ancient art' and 'artists are only modern or ancient in relation to their moment'.

This affirmation is made in the context of the dedication in *Apenas uma narrativa* (*Just a Story*), addressed to Aquilino Ribeiro, the revered Portuguese novelist who used ostensibly archaic language in his works. In *Apenas uma narrativa* António Pedro, in his own way, did the opposite: he used the experimentalist language of the 'moment' to recover the ancient picaresque tradition. He called his story 'a novel' ('*um romance*'), invoking an assertion made by another writer who sought to recover tradition in modernism, his Brazilian friend Mário de Andrade, that 'a novel is whatever its author decides to designate as such.'

António Pedro's 'novel' has been compared to two works of fiction by another Portuguese modernist poet and painter Almada Negreiros – the picaresque novel *Nome de Guerra* (*War Name*) and the surrealist short story *A Engomadeira* (*The Laundress*) – and to the Brazilian novel *Macunaíma: o heroi sem nenhum caráter* (*Macunaima: the hero without a character*) by Mário de Andrade, which is simultaneously a founding text of modern Brazilian identity and a deconstruction of this identity. There are, in fact, analogies that justify these comparisons. But I do not consider that a comparativist approach is the best way to understand the originality of António Pedro's narrative. In my view, this originality consists in the intertwining of the metaphorical and the designative in a seamless syntax that fuses the two levels of meaning. *Apenas uma narrativa* is both an autobiographical novel – specific locations, lived experiences, people remembered, loves consummated or desired, public events – and the transformation of this autobiographical material into a dream sequence. It is not a narration of dreams through the facts relating to them, as dream narratives tend to be, but an inverse transposition of lived facts into oneiric representations. It is a literary construct, which reverses the procedures of psychoanalytical methodology, moving from the conscious to the subconscious and from that threshold to an unconscious that transcends the individual. In the mythical allegory that emerges from this literary construct, Adam, the first man (Adam the Farmer), becomes a man who is all men, unfolding into a constantly changing narrator who finally changes himself into a cosmic rain.

The hero of this autobiographical narrative is not a 'subject', he's a 'predicate'. He changes shape – or name – but the characteristics that define him are recognizable in each metamorphosis. He is a picaresque anti-hero on an epic quest who goes from mythical founder of humankind, the farmer who works the land, to the 'nothingness' which simultaneously absorbs him into itself and disperses him as the impersonal rain that nourishes the earth, the water of life. If, for António Pedro theatre consists in 'making the word flesh', his 'novel' represents (also theatrically?) the reverse of that process by making flesh into word.

Helder Macedo

ACKNOWLEDGEMENTS

We wish to express our profound gratitude to José-Augusto França for encouraging us to undertake this project and granting us copyright permission. Sincere thanks are also due to Suzette and Helder Macedo, who readily provided invaluable suggestions on the English translation; to Phoebe Oliver for assistance with the translation of Bruno's article into English; to João Marques Lopes for timely information on Mário de Andrade; and to Alastair Brotchie, who kindly shared not only his expert knowledge of Surrealism but also unpublished material in his possession. In Brazil, our thanks are due to Antônio Cândido and Maria Lúcia Dal Farra. Various library and other archival collections welcomed our queries during the course of our research and we are grateful to their staff for their support. We must single out Joanne Edwards and Helen Buchanan at the Taylorian Institution, Oxford, for going beyond the call of duty and helping us to track down copies of *Clima*, and Andrea Malone, for sending the relevant PDF files. In Oxford, we thank the Faculty of Medieval and Modern Languages, the Sub-faculty of Portuguese, and Wadham College. Among colleagues and friends, we would like to record our appreciation to Prof. T. F. Earle and Dr Claire Williams, for their useful comments during the early stages of this project, and to Prof. Jonathan Thacker, as Series Editor of Hispanic Classics, for his willingness to provide a good home for António Pedro.

A NOTE ABOUT THE TRANSLATION
AND THE PRESENT EDITION

Mariana Gray de Castro's translation was guided, where appropriate, by the unpublished version produced by D. M. Evans fifty years ago. The present edition takes as its base text the first edition of *Apenas uma narrativa* (1942). A few obvious typos were corrected and the spelling was modernised, using the conventions of the Novo Acordo Ortográfico. In a few cases, however, old-fashioned orthography was maintained in keeping with the timeless effect intended by António Pedro: firstly in the case of a name like Ildebrando, a name-place like Serra d'Arga and a location like beira d'água; secondly, in 'galo galaroz, perninhas de retroz' to preserve the folk-like nature of the saying.

TRANSATLANTIC TRAVEL AND MODERNIST TRANSFORMATIONS: THE SINGULAR CASE OF *APENAS UMA NARRATIVA*

António Pedro da Costa (1909–1966), best known as António Pedro, stands out for his wide-ranging contribution to Portuguese cultural life, from the 1930s through to the 1960s, four decades deeply marked by Salazar's dictatorship.[1] His commitment to the experimental dimensions of modernity, together with his propensity to think outside the box, allowed him to thrive on the creative synergies generated by overlapping artistic interests and practices. He was involved in a truly breathtaking range of activities: as writer, he tackled all the main genres (poetry, prose and drama), but he also left his mark as a painter, a sculptor, an art critic and essayist, a journalist and radio broadcaster, and last but not least, as a theatre director, to mention only the most significant.[2] As the director of TEP (Teatro Experimental do Porto) between 1953 and 1961, he is widely acknowledged to have revolutionised the Portuguese stage, despite the growing constraints of censorship in the 1950s, and it is in this context that he remains perhaps best known today in Portugal. *Apenas uma narrativa* (1942) is probably his most successful literary achievement, where influences from different avant-gardes, encompassing France and Brazil as well as Portugal, converge and are transformed.

I. António Pedro and *Apenas uma narrativa* in Context

Twentieth century modernity had been launched in Portugal in 1915 with the magazine *Orpheu* – masterminded by the likes of Pessoa, Sá-Carneiro and Almada Negreiros.[3] If outright experimentalism took a back seat once Portugal gradually moved towards a dictatorship from 1926 onwards, in other countries a plethora of avant-gardes continued to thrive. In France, Breton's first surrealist manifesto dates from 1924, the second from 1928. Outside Europe, the Brazilian avant-garde famously staged the *Semana de Arte Moderna* in 1922, a week-long celebration of the first centenary of Brazilian independence from Portugal, and went on to propose the concept of *antropofagia* (antropophagy), the cannibalist consumption of the European coloniser's culture, with Oswald de Andrade's provocative 1928 *Manifesto Antropófago*.[4] With *Apenas uma narrativa* Pedro orchestrates a work that deftly combines and goes beyond these various experimental trends, a fact due in no small measure to the versatility of his cosmopolitan credentials. Surprisingly, his many points of contact with Brazilian Modernism have been generally overlooked until now and will therefore require particular attention in the course of our study.

1. A transnational avant-garde artist
The extent of Pedro's cosmopolitan profile and first-hand contact with European modernity as well as the Brazilian *avant-garde* places him in a fairly unusual position for a Portuguese intellectual in the first half of the 20th century. He was born in Praia, Cape Verde in 1909,[5] which he visited again in 1928–1929. A precocious teenager, his stay inspired a slim collection comprising fourteen short poems, entitled *Diário* (*Diary*), published in Praia in 1929.

He lived in Paris in 1934–1935, where he participated in avant-garde movements, met leading artists, and exhibited some of his *15 poèmes au hasard* (*15 Poems at Random*) in the salon of *Les Surindépendants* (1935). These 'dimensional' poems are Pedro's interpretation of the artistic vision embraced by Dimensionism, a movement which sought to add a new dimension to each of the arts. Aged 26, Pedro went on to become one of the co-authors of the Dimensionist manifesto, published in Paris in 1936 and signed by the likes of Arp, Robert and Sonia Delaunay, Duchamp, Kandinsky, Ben Nicholson, Miró, and Picabia, among others.[6] Back in Portugal, Pedro attempted to divulge Dimensionism, but its principles would often be confused with those of a better known school, Surrealism, founded by Breton in 1924. As a result, Pedro initially became the *de facto* representative of Surrealism, a movement which, according to Breton's second surrealist manifesto, 'aims quite simply at the total recovery of our psychic force by a means which is nothing other than the dizzying descent into ourselves, the systematic illumination of hidden places' (1972, 136–137). Surrealism would flourish in various countries in Europe throughout the 1930s and beyond, and Pedro was a precursor of the fully fledged movement in Portugal.[7]

As early as 1936, in the context of an exhibition of independent modern artists (*Exposição dos artistas modernos independentes*), he was already displaying paintings which included surrealist motifs. In 1939, in a Portuguese context where the dictatorship had been increasingly tightening its grip via censorship, Pedro defended avant-garde art in a pamphlet *Grandeza e virtudes da Arte Moderna – resposta à agressão do Sr. Ressano Garcia* (*The Virtues and Greatness of Modern Art – an answer to the attack by Mr Ressano Garcia*). The publication included complimentary references to Surrealism in response to a lecture, delivered by the President of the Sociedade Nacional das Belas Artes, which attacked modern art. It followed on from an immediate protest, when Almada Negreiros (the *enfant terrible* of Portuguese Modernism and the most representative surviving member of *Orpheu*, after the deaths of Sá-Carneiro in 1916 and Pessoa in 1935), Pedro and a few other others had sprung to their feet during the lecture itself to register their disapproval. By all accounts, they prevented the presenter from carrying on.[8] Another exhibition that same year (*4.ª Exposição de Arte Moderna*, held in the Secretariado da Propaganda Nacional quarters), continued to showcase work imbued with surrealist elements. These various gestures precede *Ex Poem*, the exhibition which is generally considered to be the first surrealist landmark proper in Portugal, organised by Pedro in Casa Repe (1940). It was Pedro's alternative to the major, dictatorship-sponsored, 1940 *Exposição do Mundo Português*, and it was arguably no coincidence that its catalogue contains a citation from Breton's first surrealist manifesto.

With these impeccable credentials linking him to European avant-garde movements, Pedro then spent another extended period abroad, this time in Brazil, where he was based for the best part of one year from December 1940 onwards, as he recounts in the autobiographical note he penned in 1955 (1979, 54). During his stay in the tropics, Pedro had the opportunity to stage two further solo exhibitions: firstly in Rio de Janeiro between 19 April and 6 May 1941, in the Museu Nacional de Belas Artes (the catalogue of which includes a brief note by the poet and visual artist Jorge de Lima);[9] and secondly in São Paulo, thanks to his contacts with the group responsible for the magazine *Clima*, from 4 Aug 1941 onwards.[10] Its catalogue featured a preface by the well-known Italian poet Giuseppe Ungaretti, then based in São Paulo.[11] Finally, in October 1941, Pedro's work was also on display in a collective exhibition, in the context of the *Salão de Arte da Feira das Indústrias*.[12]

Several contemporary newspaper interviews, copies of which are available in the Pedro archive housed in BNP (Biblioteca Nacional de Portugal), shed light on his connections with a network of key Brazilian modernists.[13] In an early interview in the Brazilian press, marking the inauguration of his first exhibition, he lists 'os culpados da minha vinda ao Brasil' ('the culprits of my coming to Brazil'). The names of those who prompted his transatlantic journey included

Adalgiso Nery, Tarsila do Amaral, Jorge de Lima, Mário de Andrade, Manuel Bandeira, Portinari, Jorge Amado, Graciliano Ramos, Lins de Rego. He adds however 'Ainda não conheci a todos pessoalmente. Já conheci outros como Murilo Mendes que estariam na lista se houvera lido em Portugal sua poesia tão misteriosa e profundamente humana' ('I haven't yet met them all in person. But I have already met others such as Murilo Mendes, who would have been on my original list if, while still in Portugal, I had read his profoundly human, mysterious poetry').[14]

The local notoriety that Pedro came to enjoy within a short amount of time of his arrival even translated into reports in the press that he had thrown a wonderful alcohol-fuelled 'surrealist' party in São Paulo, lasting into the early hours: 'E contavam que ele dera uma festa surrealista em seu apartamento onde, num terraço que dá para os arredores do Mercado Novo, pintores e artistas se divertiram, até 4 horas da madrugada, junto duma bomba de "chopp" [*sic*]' ('and we were told he had given a surrealist party in his flat where, on an open terrace overlooking the Mercado Novo, painters and artists enjoyed themselves until four o'clock in the morning, around a keg of beer').[15] The identification of Pedro as a Surrealist in this article, foregrounded in its title 'O Português surrealista', is especially eye-catching even if, as we will see, Pedro's own position on his surrealist affiliation remained rather more nuanced.

His first interview, once back in Portugal, provides a further contemporary testimonial about his extensive list of Brazilian contacts. He evokes most warmly Jorge de Lima and Jorge Amado, stressing that he also interacted with Lins do Rego, Rachel de Queiroz, Gilberto Freire (who, together with Graciliano Ramos, were major writers and public intellectuals hailing from the 1930s Brazilian North East). The interview also refers to contemporary Brazilian visual artists, stating that Segal, Portinari and Tarsila, were its greatest representatives. Tarsila do Amaral, alongside her then husband Oswald de Andrade, had been associated with the *Antropofagia* movement in 1928, and Pedro highlights that she offered 'um dos aspectos mais curiosos da pintura moderna do Mundo – o regresso à terra depois da experiência cubista' ('one of the most curious aspects of modern world painting – a return to the earth after her cubist experience').[16] This is something that would chime with Pedro's own concerns in *Apenas uma narrativa*.

From São Paulo specifically, Pedro pays tribute to a new generation of art critics 'essa pleiade de rapazes que faz o *Clima*' ('this talented group of young men who produce the magazine *Clima*'), including, among other names, its literary critic Antônio Cândido, its art critic Lourival Machado, and, as a short story writer, the university lecturer Gilda de Morais Rocha.[17] Antônio Cândido would go on to become one of the best-known and most influential Brazilian literary critics of the 20th century and, as will be seen shortly, his reviews of Pedro's work contain information which sheds new light of the gestation of *Apenas uma narrativa.*

Last but not least, Pedro underlines to his Portuguese interviewer the importance of Mário de Andrade and Oswald de Andrade, key players in the 1922 São Paulo Semana de Arte Moderna. Crucially for our purposes, we are told that Mário: 'é não só o autor de "Macunaíma", a mais interessante fantasmagoria que se publicou em português [...], como é, a justos títulos, o crítico e o mentor da juventude' ('Not only is he the author of *Macunaíma*, the most interesting phantasmagoric work written in Portuguese [...] but he is also, by rights, the critic and the mentor of the younger generation').[18] Evidence of Pedro's regard for Mário de Andrade can also be found in the 1941 Brazilian press interviews. Most surprisingly, one interview reveals that 'Um dos seus grandes sonhos é há muitos anos fazer o "Macunaíma", de Mário de Andrade, em desenho animado. Mas não passou de projeto' ('For many years one of his big dreams has been to produce an animated version of Mário de Andrade's *Macunaíma.* But it remained only a project').[19] Pedro's visionary predisposition stands out here, for indeed a film of *Macunaíma* would eventually be made (1969). For his part, Mário also publicly recognized Pedro's artistic merit in a detailed and broadly favourable appraisal of his paintings, despite a number of reservations.[20] Their friendship is further confirmed by the presence, in Mário de Andrade's archives in São Paulo, of three unpublished letters that Pedro addressed to him, as well as a small painting by Pedro.[21]

In short, Pedro's first-hand interaction with a vibrant Brazilian cultural scene is likely to have left some traces in *Apenas uma narrativa,* a novella published just a few months after his return from Brazil. Yet, while critics have duly highlighted Pedro's affinities with French Surrealism in general and with Breton in particular, Pedro's tantalising engagement with the creativity of the ground-breaking *Macunaíma* has been, to the best of my knowledge, so far almost entirely overlooked by criticism, especially on the Portuguese side, a fact perhaps explicable by the fact that the first Portuguese edition of *Macunaíma* only came out in 1998.[22] Before exploring how various reverberations of Brazilian Modernism are woven into the fabric of *Apenas uma narrativa,* the broader literary canvas for the emergence of Pedro's pioneer text should be considered.

2. The Gestation of Apenas uma narrativa

In terms of gestation, there is evidence to suggest that the novella was composed over a period of several years. In particular, Chapter V was published almost in its entirety (with the notable exception of the last two paragraphs) in a Portuguese magazine in 1939, with the curious label of 'conto irracional' ('irrational short story') (Pedro 1939).[23] Even more curious is the bracketed information that follows, which indicates that the tale belonged to the 'livro em preparação *Antropofagia e outros contos*' ('*Antropophagy and Other Tales*, in preparation') (Appendix 1). In other words, it suggests that the notion of Antropophagy was already imprinted on Pedro's consciousness *prior* to his stay in Brazil. It is of course possible, given his markedly cosmopolitan profile, that he had already come across Oswald de Andrade's *Manifesto Antropófago* (1928) by then. That said, the familiarity of Pedro with the concept of cannibalism can also be explained through his direct contact with the artistic avant-garde in Paris during the mid 1930s. After all, Pedro was one of the signatories of the aforementioned 1935 *Manifeste Dimensioniste*, alongside important names such as Picabia, whose own *Manifeste Cannibale* dated back to 1920 and was subsequently devoured by Oswald by his own admission.[24] On a related note, it is possible to find cannibalistic motifs in various pictures of the 1930s such as Dali's 1936 *Autumn Cannibalism*, and this trend is also present in some of Pedro's own paintings completed prior to his stay in Brazil, in particular *O Repasto Imundo* (1939) (*Revolting Meal*) (Appendix 2), where the central figure appears to be about to feast on a dish of eyes, or *A Paz Inquieta* (1940) (*Troubled Peace*), where a woman seems about to sink her teeth into the leg of a domineering man.

A vital piece of information regarding the composition of *Apenas uma narrativa* can be found in Antônio Cândido's early review of the novella for *Clima* (1942). In his opening paragraph, the critic indicates that Pedro had read out some extracts to him. This must have taken place during Pedro's stay in 1941, in other words prior to the publication in book form. Cândido also mentions that he had furthermore received a typescript of these 'narrativas' ('stories') (1942, 88). His recurrent use of the plural suggests that this is not a typo, leading us to believe that the extracts and stories that Cândido encountered were probably from the book in preparation, initially called *Antropofagia e outros contos*. We can postulate, then, that this collection only remained unpublished because it was subsequently recycled as a pre-text for *Apenas uma narrativa*. The fact that the independent short narratives that Cândido had come across in 1941 subsequently acquired a unifying thread in *Apenas uma narrativa* is highlighted by the critic, who states that the work 'aparece *agora* construída segundo um nexo subitamente tão claro pela ligação operada entre as suas partes' ('*now* appears constructed according to connections suddenly made obvious through the linking of different parts') (p. 90, my italics). In those circumstances, it is hardly surprising that Cândido's review stresses above all the artistic lucidity of Pedro 'que lembra, no delírio, a realidade mais alta do artista ordenador' ('which recalls, in delirium, the higher reality of the artist who organizes') (p. 91).[25] Even though Cândido falls short of stating it, perhaps the transformation of the short stories as they coalesced into a whole may help us to understand the title better. For, if we think about it, in its final published version, there is after all only a single narrative – in other words just *one* narrative – and no longer a series of freestanding tales.

The fact that Pedro was a keen practitioner of short stories at that point in time is further corroborated by a one-page prose piece published during his stay in Brazil, in April 1941, which stylistically and thematically seems a precursor to the fully fledged text of *Apenas uma narrativa*. It is entitled 'Última folha de um diário de viagem' ('Last page of a travel diary') and dedicated 'Ao Jorge de Lima' (Appendix 3).[26] The opening sentence alludes to Pedro's arrival in Rio: 'Quando eu cheguei à cidade rolou-me a cabeça nos pináculos e nos vales e foi um espectáculo maravilhoso' ('When I arrived to the city, my head rolled on the summits and vales and it was a wonderful spectacle').[27] It goes on to mention Carnival and the iconic statue of Christ at the top of the Corcovado. Its closing paragraph reads retrospectively almost like a preliminary version of *Apenas uma narrativa*, conflating both the fate of the planter Adam in the opening chapter and that of the protagonist himself in the closing one:

Sabes? Depois desta viagem só poderei fazer outra viagem. Sinto já nos ossos meu cansaço de fim de mundo e aqui este sol vai amadurecer-me a carne por completo. Depois será lindíssimo o meu fim. Hei-de procurar uma planície sem sombras. Hei-de plantar-me no meio, enorme, como uma doença da terra. Depois escorregar-me-ão as feições até ao chão. Ficarei aí como uma mancha até às primeiras chuvas. Se vieres por esse tempo colhe num vaso alguns torrões. Devem servir para fazer crescer as orquídeas e os fetos.

(You know what? After this journey I can't but undertake another journey. I already feel in my bones an end of the world weariness and, here, this sun is going to ripen my flesh completely. Then my ending will be exquisite. I will seek out a plain devoid of shade. I will plant myself in the middle, enormous, like an illness of the earth. Then my features will slide into the ground. There I will remain like a stain until the first rains. If you come by around this time, please gather some earth in a vase. It should prove useful for growing orchids and baby fern).[28]

The title chosen for this piece, the final entry in a travel diary, brings to mind the title of the 1929 Cape Verdean collection *Diário*. As such, it may hint at the completion of a cycle. And indeed, with the benefit of hindsight, it could be argued that the statement in the closing paragraph: 'Depois desta viagem só poderei fazer outra viagem' announces Pedro's next journey – the one embodied in *Apenas uma narrativa*, which would take place in Portugal itself: a modern *viagem na minha terra* (journey in my homeland) of sorts, to recall the title of Garrett's famous novel, published almost exactly one century earlier.[29]

It is also worth pointing out that at least one of Pedro's paintings produced while in Brazil, *Quando Cristo vira estrela* (*When Christ Becomes a Star*), seems to have succinctly tackled some of the key themes subsequently developed in *Apenas uma narrativa*. Not unlike the short tale dedicated to Jorge de Lima, it too appears to conflate images present in the opening and closing chapter. Although unfortunately the painting in question appears to have been lost, we know for sure that it was exhibited in Rio, because it is listed in the catalogue, and in São Paulo, because Mário de Andrade's critical appraisal singles out its 'sincronizações luminosas [que] me agradam francamente' ('luminous synchronisations which I found frankly pleasing'), and its 'primeiro plano, verdadeiro achado' ('foreground, a real find').[30] The painting was subsequently displayed in a Portuguese exhibition and a review clarifies what we already suspected from its title, namely that the theme depicted was based on the iconic Rio landmark of the Corcovado Christ: 'A realidade foi testemunhada de forma desassossegada. A fantasmagoria duma noite brasileira foi sentida com certa exaltação imaginativa, sendo naturalmente espontânea a tentação de assemelhar o Corcovado iluminado ao restante brilho estelar.' ('Reality was witnessed with disquiet. The fantasy of a Brazilian night was experienced with a degree of delirious imagination, leading to the natural temptation of comparing the illuminated Corcovado Christ to the rest of the shining stars').[31] Armed with the information that the gigantic statue of Christ, inaugurated in 1931, provided the starting-point for *Quando Cristo vira estrela*, one might detect a trace of the famous Corcovado Christ in the illustration of the opening chapter of *Apenas uma narrativa*, representing Adam. Although Adam, a planter endowed with a biblical name, does not have outstretched arms, he does spectacularly self-combust soon after.[32] Moreover, if we fast forward to the closing chapter of *Apenas uma narrativa*, we are faced with another possible link to *Quando Cristo vira estrela*, when the unnamed narrator unexpectedly collides with a star and likewise catches fire, described as 'como um fogo de artifício' ('like a firework display').

In a nutshell, the meaningful linking of the different parts of *Apenas uma narrativa* seems to have been prompted by Pedro's stay in Brazil. Certainly, two of the pieces he completed in the first half of his time there, the short text 'Última folha de um diário de viagem', and the painting *Quando Cristo vira estrela*, seem to provide snapshots of some of the novella's inaugural and parting images, perhaps paving the way for a 'framing' that allows the artistic sum becomes more than its parts. It may not be entirely a coincidence that one is a text and one is an image for, significantly, the final version of *Apenas uma narrativa* is illustrated, a fact that adds further depth to the work as a whole.

3. Literary Landscape
Apenas uma narrativa was published in early 1942.[33] Writing against the backdrop of an unfolding World War II, during which Salazar's Portugal would remain officially neutral, Pedro was able to produce a work containing oblique references to a war-ridden and politically-charged context. He achieved this by alternating intentionally between a realist and fantastic style. This strategy distinguished him from most of his contemporaries in Portugal. Indeed, throughout the 1940s neorealism – as social realism became known in a Portuguese context – a socially engaged movement, became the prevailing literary school.[34] In a cultural context shaped by the emergence of neorealism, *Apenas uma narrativa*, alongside the earlier *Nome de guerra* by the modernist Almada Negreiros, was neglected by criticism precisely because both stood, as José-Augusto França convincingly shows, as works which did not fit the mould of Portuguese novelistic production of the first half of the 20th century (1986, 159). While *Apenas uma narrativa* only enjoyed one edition in Pedro's own lifetime, he was fully conscious of its innovative dimension, to the extent that he concluded his preface by recommending 'por modéstia obrigatória, sem nenhuma convicção' ('with the obligatory modesty, and with no conviction') that his readers need not read his work. In fact, as Bruno Silva Rodrigues' research authoritatively uncovers in the article that follows, Pedro was not only willing to share his tale with members of the London surrealist group, but also interested in securing its dissemination in English translation.

While *Apenas uma narrativa* has generally been received as an example of surrealist prose,[35] it is important to note that in the early 1940s Pedro did not subscribe to Surrealism wholesale. In fact, he expressed some reservations, succinctly encapsulated by the following statement, made in the course of an interview in Brazil in 1941:

O grande apport surrealista, como já disse uma vez, foi a descoberta da sub-
consciência que o automatismo revelava, e, por ela e por ele, o grande encontro do
Homem na magia dos seus símbolos. [...] O que mais me separa dos surrealistas
é a aceitação do fato 'Arte', com todas as suas consequências: controle da
inteligência na associação das imagens, aceitação e estudo dos processos técnicos
tradicionais, isto é do resultado da cultura pictural, que os surrealistas, pelo menos
teoricamente negam e condenam como restricção à livre expressão individual. O
que deles me aproxima é o sonho, os dados irracionais como ponto de partida, é
o encanto sobre as coisas duma imaginação baroquisante, delirante se for preciso
e possível, a única faculdade do espírito que, com certeza, só o homem possui à
face da terra.

The great contribution of Surrealism, as I have stated previously, was the discovery
of the sub-conscious revealed by automatic writing and, thanks to both these
mechanisms, the great encounter of Man in the magic of symbols. That which
separates me most from Surrealists is my willingness to accept 'Art' as a fact, with
all its resulting consequences: the control of intelligence over image association,
the acceptance and study of conventional technical devices, in other words the
outcome of pictorial culture, which Surrealists, at least theoretically, deny and
condemn as a limitation on individual free expression. That which draws me
close to them is dream, irrational data as a starting-point; it is the charm that a
baroque-like imagination, delirious if necessary and possible, confers on things;
surely the only property of the mind that man alone possesses on the face of
earth.[36]

In keeping with these assertions, Pedro's adoption of core principles of
Surrealism in *Apenas uma narrativa* is selective. Moreover, the prolonged
gestation of the novella confirms the extent to which he accepted 'the fact of art
with all its resulting consequences'. Nonetheless, against a background shaped
by a regimented dictatorship, there is, unsurprisingly, an intention to propose
an alternative to the prevailing rational and logical mode. As Pedro himself
highlights in his preface: 'A história que vai ler-se é simples como as plantas
e nasceu como elas naturalmente, embora, como elas, tenha por vezes formas
inesperadas. Não tem intenção de provar coisa nenhuma mas, se a tivesse, seria
a de que há uma lógica do absurdo tão verdadeira, pelo menos, como a lógica
racional' ('The story that follows is as simple as plants and was born, like plants,
naturally, even though, like plants, it sometimes takes on surprising shapes. It
does not aim to prove anything but, if it did, it would be to prove that there
exists a logic of the absurd that is as true as rational logic'). The praise of the
logic of absurdity as a starting-point clearly aligns Pedro with one of the main

surrealist tenets. It is also pertinent to note at this juncture that, following his stay in Paris in the mid-1930s, Pedro would in fact maintain contact with Breton, as stated in his autobiography, where he claims that the leader of the French surrealist movement always sent him his latest books (1979, 56). It is likely therefore that he was familiar with Breton's main surrealist prose-works, including *Nadja* which dates from 1928 and *L'Amour fou*, published in 1937. The various experimental journeys undergone by the protagonist in *Apenas uma narrativa* entail an exploration which, in many ways, mirrors the surrealist intention of recovering the psychic forces of the unconscious. As Alçada (1982) postulates, the serependitous encounter between the narrator and Lulu may be indebted to the concept of *hasard objectif* (objective chance) defined in *L'Amour fou* as '*la forme de manifestation de la nécessité extérieure qui se fraie un chemin dans l'inconscient humain*' (Breton [1937] 1988, vol II, 690, italics in the original) ('the form of manifestation of an external necessity which finds a way into the human unconscious').

But, notwithstanding Pedro's acceptance of unconscious necessity, the novella is not entirely chaotic: it remains a conscious work of art in terms of composition and design, structured into ten short chapters and furthermore features a complex interplay between text and illustrations. In fact, Pedro's deliberate and self-conscious artistic composition means that, from the outset, the inclusion of several paratexts frames the reader's interpretation of the novella.

4. Paratexts

Two of the paratexts which frame the novella explicitly pay tribute to Pedro's Portuguese lineage: the modernist Mário de Sá-Carneiro (1890–1916) provides the epigraph, while the work itself is dedicated to Aquilino Ribeiro (1885–1963). A third explicit acknowledgement, located within the preface, is a statement attributed to Mário de Andrade (1893–1945).

Pedro publicly acknowledged his debt to the *Orpheu* generation on more than one occasion: for instance the aforementioned *Exposição dos artistas modernos independentes*, in 1936, was dedicated to two of its leading visual artists, Amadeo de Souza-Cardoso and Santa-Rita Pintor, and two writers, Mário de Sá-Carneiro and Fernando Pessoa, the latter only recently deceased. Incidentally, the label chosen by Sá-Carneiro for *A Confissão de Lúcio* (*Lucio's Confession*) – a 1914 novella permeated with fantastic elements which could be seen as a surrealist text *avant la lettre* – had been precisely *narrativa*. The epigraph of *Apenas uma narrativa* comes from one of Sá-Carneiro's quirky sonnets, 'El-Rei' ('His Majesty'): 'Meu Dislate a conventos longos orça' (1996, 140) ('My Folly to lengthy cloisters amounts'), an enigmatic line given the indeterminacy of its symbolist imagery. Existential estrangement or exile was a recurring theme in Sá-Carneiro.[37] One cannot help feeling that Pedro's choice of an epigraph which obliquely deals with estrangement is especially telling, given his return only a few months earlier to Portugal after his transatlantic experience. On a personal level, we may speculate that *Apenas uma narrativa* acts as Pedro's attempt, through a process of literary symbolization, to come to terms with the complex task of re-engaging with his Portuguese roots. In this context, it is interesting to note that, following yet another stay abroad, in London in 1944–5, his definitive return to Portugal would see him eventually moving away from Lisbon, from the early 1950s onwards, in order to base himself in Moledo do Minho (in other words next door to Caminha, which provides the setting for most of *Apenas uma narrativa*).

By contrast, Pedro feels the need to justify more fully his dedication to the novelist Aquilino which, on the surface, may indeed seem unexpected insofar as the latter belonged to an older generation. Aquilino, praised by him for children's books like the classic *Romance da raposa* (*Novel of the Fox*) (1924) or *Arca de Noé* (*Noah's Ark*) (1936), often drew on his rural roots. Unlike the more aristocratic posture cultivated by the modernist Sá-Carneiro, he understood ordinary people, with whom Pedro can also be seen to empathise at various junctures in *Apenas uma narrativa*. Thus, Pedro highlights that Aquilino was modern in relation to his time, by enacting 'a volta à terra depois da especulação, a volta ao gosto infantil depois da pedagogia parva, a volta ao sonho e à epopeia depois da crítica e da caricatura' ('the return to earth after speculation, the return to childish pleasures after foolish pedagogy, the return to dreams and epics after criticism and caricature'). The keywords here (return to earth, childish pleasures, dreams and epics) all resonate on some level with what Pedro sets out to achieve with *Apenas uma narrativa*.

Last but not least, in a third paratextual element, the preface, Pedro invokes the authority of Mário de Andrade, rather than any European luminary such as Breton, as might have been expected, given Portugal's adulation of French culture at the time. Pedro claims that the pope of Brazilian Modernism had put a timely stop to the endless debate about what might qualify as a novel, when he wisely stated that the author should always have the final word: 'Romance é aquilo que o seu autor resolveu designar assim' ('A novel is something its author decided to call a novel'). This assertion, designed to settle the question of genre once and for all, accordingly enabled Pedro to label his 'story' as a novel. But it is hard not to see a parodic intention in Pedro's (possibly apocryphal) citation of Andrade given that, in practice, the latter had in fact used his authorial prerogative to avoid bestowing the title of 'romance' upon *Macunaíma*. He settled instead for the label 'rhapsody', and only belatedly from the second edition (1937) onwards (Lopez 1978, XXII and XIX). Still, the citation effectively links *Apenas uma narrativa* and its author with the Brazilian *avant-garde* rather than with Breton. It is therefore worth dwelling briefly on what aspects Pedro may have drawn from *Macunaíma*, over and above *Nadja*, two prose-works coincidentally published in 1928.

Breton began *Nadja* with the rhetorical question 'Qui suis-je?' (1988, vol. I, 646) ('Who am I?'), pointing to the presence of an underlying quest motif throughout. On the surface, Pedro's tale appears to offer likewise an individual journey. However, as an intellectual from the cultural semi-periphery, Pedro could not avoid engaging with and negotiating issues of nationness, a trait he shared with Andrade. Both Lusophone tales follow a similar pattern, stretching as they do from the birth of their respective protagonist to the moment when each returns to his hometown, to meet his final transformation/demise, after multiple picaresque adventures and mind-blowing episodes. Admittedly, Mário de Andrade was rather more explicitly concerned with the collective import of his 'rhapsody' than Pedro, as is plain from his incipit 'No fundo do mato-virgem nasceu Macunaíma, herói de *nossa gente*' (my italics) ([1937] 1978, 7) ('In the depths of the virgin forest, Macunaima, the hero of *our* people, was born').[38] Unlike Andrade, Pedro settles for a first-person voice after his opening chapter, which lends a more subjective feel to the Portuguese *narrativa* – as was the case with *Nadja*. It must be noted, however, that an important consideration might have persuaded Pedro to opt for predominant use of a first-person narrative: the need to throw censorship off the scent in a loaded dictatorship context. Certainly, in his playfulness and the constant lacing of *Apenas uma narrativa* with parody, Pedro is unquestionably on the same wavelength as Andrade.

Broadly speaking, one might say the characteristics that Pedro appropriates from *Macunaíma* are its delirious (surreal) atmosphere, which also occurs in Breton's *Nadja*, and its humorous and satirical tone, which does not. Like his Brazilian counterpart, Pedro relishes laughing at established conventions. For instance, in the opening chapter, he pokes fun at the typecast reaction of the members of the Academy when confronted with the inexplicable shadow left by the planter: they duly pen a series of commemorative sonnets (a traditional poetic-form par excellence). Their production is the butt of another dig in the next sentence, when it is wryly contrasted with his own veridic tale: 'Desse conjunto de produções literárias da melhor água se fez e se editou um livro que aí corre e não tem, evidentemente, nada de comum com esta história verdadeira' ('Those first-rate literary productions were put in a book which still survives and does not have, of course, anything to do with this true story'). In fact, the slippery boundaries between fact and fiction, as we will now go on to analyse in more detail, permeate the text from beginning to end.

II. Thematic Strands in *Apenas uma narrativa*

It seems reasonable to assume that the open letter that Pedro wrote to Aquilino, to whom he dedicated his 'novel', was one of the finishing touches to *Apenas uma narrativa*, since it only dates from November 1941. Of particular interest for our purposes are the words that Pedro used to describe what he viewed as Aquilino's overriding themes – namely a return to earth, childish pleasures, dreams and epics – for these are connected to the novella's main thematic preoccupations in one way or another. We will therefore draw loosely on related strands to anchor our discussion and consider the implications of, firstly, the all-pervasive oneiric atmosphere and its underlying link with the uncanny; secondly, the presence of mock-epic, given the parody of both myths of origin and 'happy ever after' endings; thirdly, the swift escalation from playful delight in the nonsensical to anthropophagic imagery; and last but not least, the return to earth and cyclical transformation.

1. Between Fantasy and Reality

Apenas uma narrativa hovers between dream and reality. In the opening chapter, for instance, an idyllic rural landscape, by a meandering river, located in lush Minho, is described in an instantly familiar realist mode through the eyes of an omniscient narrator. Nonetheless, this misleadingly 'normal' incipit soon veers into unfamiliar territory, thanks to a deeply disturbing take on the Biblical genesis account (an unavoidable association given the name Adam, ascribed to the planter at the outset, in the caption featured below the illustration): not only is Eve nowhere to be seen but by the second paragraph the text reinforces the symbolism conveyed by the illustration, as Adam is depicted as carrying and sowing mutilated female body parts, in an ironic distortion of the biblical account of divine creation. As Rodrigues (2013) convincingly shows, such instability and blurring of boundaries produces an unsettling effect, what Freud refers to as *the uncanny*. In the words of Freud, the narrator effectively 'tricks us by promising us everyday reality and then going beyond it. We react to his fictions as if they had been our own experiences. By the time we become aware of the trickery, it is too late: the writer has already done what he set out to do' (2003, 157).

The opening of Chapter II, like that of the incipit, strikes a surface realist note in its description of Caminha. But the realm of fantasy soon takes over from reality again, as the protagonist becomes embroiled in impossible adventures: in a flooded house, surrounded by apocalyptic destruction, his limbs fall off and he can only escape by building a (childlike) paper boat. This offers a surreal take on another well-known Bible story, that of Noah's ark. The parody is clear given that, unlike Noah, the young hero is very much on his own. And, taking its cue from these two opening chapters, indeterminacy between an oneiric world and the real one continues to permeate the remainder of the narrative.

Other, arguably even more disturbing, configurations of the uncanny stem from links between sexuality and the monstrous. In Chapter III, the desiring male gazes which objectify the beautiful Lulu are kept in check as she 'collects' eyes and keeps them safely boxed. The fear of losing one's eyesight was discussed by Freud, in connection with Hoffman's *The Sandman* as a fear of castration and is consequently another element that triggers the uncanny.

Most notably, in a subsequent dream-like episode in Chapter VIII, conventional idealised beauty is soon shattered and acquires uncanny attributes, perhaps following the footsteps of the final sentence of *Nadja* ('La beauté sera CONVULSIVE ou ne sera pas' (1988, vol. 1, 753) ('Beauty will be CONVULSIVE or will not be at all'). An unnamed virginal woman, initially described as 'Ela apareceu-me vestida de branco e linda a oferecer-se-me' ('She appeared dressed in white, beautiful, offering herself to me'), morphs into a predator, when her eyes turn into monstrous sexual organs that threaten to devour the narrator: 'Do buraco dos olhos saíam-lhe bichos gordos que depois inchavam desmedidamente. Pareciam sexos e, como ela, era para mim que sorriam. [...] Ela queria continuar a beijar-me mas os bichos comiam-me os olhos até que me foi possível morder um, cheio duma raiva que me possuiu todo. Fiquei cheio de sangue e de medo' ('From her empty eye sockets fat slugs crept out, that kept on swelling. They looked like sexual parts and they smiled at me, as she did. [...] She wanted to carry on kissing me but the slugs ate my eyes until I managed to bite one, full of a fury that possessed me completely. I was left bloody and terrified'). Once more, then, the woman becomes endowed with castrating properties, and the blurring of dream and reality provokes an uncanny effect.

Such effect may be compounded by a sense of *déjà vu*. In this connection, it is worth noting that this cannibalistic sexual encounter takes place in a faraway exotic land, Mexico, which may stand in, through Freudian displacement, for Brazil. Certainly, there seems to be an echo here of Tarsila do Amaral's most famous painting, *Abaporu*, credited with having inspired Oswald de Andrade to pen his *Manifesto Antropófago*.[39] The description of the landscape reads almost like an ekphrasis of her striking picture, which portrayed a solitary primitive figure, with a huge cactus and sun in the background: 'Sei que me parecia no México, onde nunca estive, por causa dos cactos e do sol' ('I know it seemed like Mexico, where I have never been, because of the cacti and the sun').

2a. (Un)homely Beginnings and Endings

If Macunaíma's collective symbolic significance starts at birth, the origins of the unnamed Portuguese protagonist are similarly steeped in a mythical, although more obviously incredible, lineage: following Adam self-combustion, the town of Caminha comes into being, and, in due course, becomes the birthplace of the first-person narrator. Homi Bhabha famously commented that 'nations, like narratives, lose their origins in the myths of time and only fully encounter their horizons in the mind's eye' (1990, 3). Here, Caminha's antecedents (and, by extension, those of the protagonist it engenders) are presented as a case of eerie begetting, likewise encapsulating the incongruities of myths of origin.[40] Lest this should be lost on the reader, Pedro closes the opening chapter with the following comment about Adam, which makes abundantly clear that his was a false start, thereby undoing the account in Genesis: 'Não é, no entanto, verdade que fosse o primeiro homem. Antes e depois dele já havia este sabor a vazio que enche o mundo duma inquietação sem remédio' ('He was not, however, the first man. Before and after him there was already this empty feeling that fills the world with an endless restlessness').

As for Caminha, although northern Portugal is inextricably associated with the creation of Portugal, the location for the cradle of the nation is traditionally considered to be Guimarães, not Caminha. Furthermore, what the text describes as Caminha's perennial sadness undermines any sense of the birth of a glorious nation. In the late nineteenth century, the north had featured prominently in Eça de Queirós' later novels: *A Ilustre Casa de Ramires* (*The Illustrious House of*

Ramires) in particular provided a in-depth reflection on Portuguese 'nationness': its opening chapter showed the paralysing effect of the weight of history on an aristocratic bachelor. A similar sense of fossilization is explicitly and irreverently conveyed by Pedro, when we are told that the protagonist's ancestral stately home 'cheirava sempre a todos os mortos que estiveram cerimoniosamente lá dentro, em câmara ardente, desde a fundação da monarquia' ('It always smelt of the dead people who had once ceremoniously been inside, lying in state, since the foundation of the monarchy'). In other words, pushing Eça de Queirós' premises to their logical conclusion, through parody, Pedro negates the possibility of a foundational narrative. Given the rigidity of the structures of a dictatorship firmly in place by the early 1940s, parody may be deployed as a means of challenging the hegemony of a status quo based on a nationalistic ideology, confirmed by grand public displays such as the 1940 Exposição do Mundo Português.

Alongside parody, modernist fluidity may similarly call into question monolithic identities and undermine any epic nationalistic discourse. Throughout the novella, the protagonist undergoes a series of transformations and nowhere is this more apparent than in Chapter IV. There, his metamorphoses are detailed in a breathtakingly long enumeration, which occupies almost two pages. The list may constitute an example of surrealist practice, a kind of automatic writing, or more precisely semi-automatism in the words of José-Augusto França (1965, 29). It may also take its cue from the vertiginous plurality of the self previously textualised by the modernist generation, not least through the remarkable case of Pessoa/Álvaro de Campos. However, the Portuguese hero's successive incarnations also link him once more to his literary forerunner, Macunaíma, whose multiple transformations pointed to the hybridity of Brazil itself.

Transformations are also highly visible in the closing chapter, depicting the final metamorphoses of the protagonist. In-between two 'surreal' moments, which shall be discussed in greater detail in a subsequent section, another list is inserted in the last but one paragraph — this time explicitly tinged with social criticism as it foregrounds 'all the world's sufferings'. Its contents are undoubtedly anchored in a historically recognizable 1940s 'here and now': 'as inundações e as guerras, o medo dos fantasmas e a maldade dos homens, aquele cheiro de arroto de certas bocas que só comem o suor dos miseráveis, aquela tristeza de flor quebrada que apodreceu num monturo, aquele pst das prostitutas, [...] os generais, a morte' ('the floods and wars, the fear of ghosts and the cruelty of men, the smell of burps from certain mouths that only feed on the sweat of the penniless, the sadness of a broken flower decaying on a rubbish heap, the psst of prostitutes, [...] the generals, death'). As such, Pedro seems to have taken advantage of the flexible boundaries between fact and fiction that he had so cleverly manipulated from the outset, to underline a string of unsavoury social and political realities, predicated not only on natural causes such as floods, but also on man-made evils such as war or socio-economic inequality.

2b. Social (Dis)order

In a regimented dictatorship context, built on a narrowly prescriptive view of 'Deus, Pátria, Família' (God, Homeland, Family), it is small wonder that Pedro adopts a dissident perspective through the use of a mock-epic narrative mode. And, if the concept of the nation comes under scrutiny and begins to unravel in *Apenas uma narrativa*, so too does the family ideology enshrined by the dictatorship.

Beneath the cover of the absurd and the uncanny, asymmetrical power relations are shown to pervade society. In Chapter V, for instance, urban industrialization seems to exacerbate the social divide. Social tensions lead to a strike – euphemistically labelled a 'motim' (disturbance, riot) in the Portuguese original, freestanding version, possibly owing to the regime's political sensitivity to strikes in late 1930s and early 1940s. In an urban landscape informed by inequality, the violent behaviour of Ildebrando – branded a thief, giving the lie to his prominent medals – stands out. Intent on having his wicked way with desirable young girls, he proceeds to metaphorically deflower them: 'espetar o alfinete de cada medalha no umbigo de cada menina para que, sobre aquela alvura, o brilho das medalhas, com suas fitas encarnadas, parecesse em cada ventre uma ferida' ('stick the pin of each medal in the bellybutton of each girl so that the glean of the medals with their scarlet ribbons looked like a wound on each tummy').

The disempowered position of vulnerable young women, gruesomely objectified (or nothing short of crucified) in this chapter, may shed light on the earlier ambiguous portrayal of alluring Lulu as a collector of admiring male gazes, in Chapter III. Margarido points out how Lulu's behaviour functions as the symptom of a necessarily virginal young woman in the ultimately perverse patriarchal context of 1930s and 1940s Portugal, with its prohibitions surrounding sexuality, especially female sexuality: not only does she effectively conforms to social expectations by not allowing herself to surrender to male desire, moreover, on a symbolic level, she castrates all the men who desire her (1988, 44–45). Certainly, the dire consequences of privileging (the eye of) one potential suitor over all others are graphically captured when the chosen eye cannot contain its excitement and explodes, staining her dress and ruining it. Needless to say, such a stain can be read both literally and figuratively.

It is surely a disruption of prevailing expectations, then, that the narrator only meets and declares his love for Lulu *after,* metaphorically speaking, she is no longer a virgin. Their passionate encounter in a cheap boarding-house at the close of Chapter III, flaunting all accepted notions of appropriate courtship, enacts a liberating temporary foray into the pleasure principle. Significantly, however, it is later overruled by 'reality' seemingly re-asserting itself, after the protagonist's second love letter to Lulu (Chapter VIII) is misread as a 'homely' marriage proposal by the young girl's well-to-do family. This is a deeply ironic twist given that, as we have seen, its contents actually transmitted the protagonist's sexual proclivities, and culminated in supremely 'unhomely' erotic experiences.

The description of the socially sanctioned union with Lulu, moreover, allows Pedro to leap at the chance to lampoon bourgeois expectations through his witty description of the wedding banquet in Chapter IX. To give but one example, the mother of the bride, so nervous that she turns into a liquid, can only partake in the proceedings held together inside a bladder. Her prepossessing husband then attempts to serve his thoroughly objectified wife as an aperitif, in a further instance of asymmetrical gendered relations which call into question the notion of a traditional happy 'ever after'. Once more, the 'homely' becomes the 'unhomely', especially when the guests' hunger knows no bounds and, shedding social propriety and restraint, they all proceed to consume each other at the end of the wedding meal. Their cannibalist behaviour emphasises the impossibility of regulating the body, given the Portuguese double meaning of the word 'comer' (to eat), which has sexual connotations. However, since this scene is also one of the several instances of anthropophagic imagery in *Apenas uma narrativa*, it may also point to an appropriation of Brazilian Modernism, as the next section attempts to uncover in more detail.

3. The Art of Cannibalism

In the wedding reception episode, the tone is predominantly satirical. By contrast, Chapter VII unfolds into a complex series of multilayered pictorial and cannibalistic allusions and therefore warrants our careful consideration.

The protagonist climbs the Arga, a mount near Caminha, in search of what he describes as 'sky' and 'God' (a search reminiscent of Macunaíma's own quest towards the end). At the top, he finds a temple but, instead of an altar, there is a

screen onto which a blonde woman is projected. According to Alçada, the screen
may suggest intertextuality with Breton's *L'Amour fou*, which contained a reference
to a screen: 'Cet écran existe. [...] Sur cet écran tout ce que l'homme veut savoir
est écrit en lettres phosphorescentes, en lettres de *désir*.' (vol. II, 754, italics in
original) ('This screen exists. [...] Everything man wants to know is written on
this screen in phosphorescent letters, in letters of desire'). Nonetheless, since
Pedro's screen is explicitly described as a cinema screen, it must be read above all
as a symbol of modernity, incongruously juxtaposed with two images associated
with European old world culture and civilization: firstly a mapa-mundi, which
occupies the floor of the central nave, and secondly a fifteenth century painting
by Andrea Mantegna, the *Lamentation of the Dead Christ*, found in a box at the
back of the cathedral-like temple. The pervasive sense of uncanny is heightened
by an ekphrasis of Mantegna's masterpiece, which stresses its supremely unfamiliar
('estranhíssima') depiction of Christ: 'Aquele quadro de Mantegna que tem um
Cristo Morto na estranhíssima postura que se conhece. Os pés enchem todo o
primeiro plano e, depois, tudo se estreita, cabendo em pouquíssimo espaço, por
causa da deformação da perspectiva, o corpo todo até à cabeça, quase no intervalo
dos pés' ('that painting by Mantegna of a dead Christ in that curious position we
are all familiar with. The feet fill the entire foreground and then the body tapers
back until, owing to deformation of perspective, the whole body up to the head
is almost contained in the space between the two feet').[41]

In a further uncanny doubling, the picture hangs inside a box, inside which
there is another box, home to two painters 'gêmeos e iguais, ambos pintores e
pederastas' ('two identical twin brothers, both painters and pederasts'). Their
paintings are mirror images of each other, and as such, one might surmise,
effectively devoid of individual originality. The twins' subservience to the Italian
master is highlighted through a humorous description: 'Em certa ocasião, um dos
irmãos levantou-se e foi lamber a palma dos pés do quadro de Mantegna' ('On
one occasion, one of the brothers stood up and went to lick the soles of the feet
in Mantegna's painting'). By this point, the increasingly eerie atmosphere takes
on a distinctly anthropophagic complexion, as one sibling kills off the blonde
woman and consumes half of her body, leaving his twin to eat up the remaining
half. If, on the one hand, the image may play yet again on the Portuguese
double meaning of the word 'comer' (to eat), on the other, on a symbolic level,
the cannibalistic behaviour of the two fair twins, described as 'so blond they
were almost ginger' (*i.e.* European-looking), may be seen through the lens of
Brazilian *antropofagia*. It would seem that here Pedro is not only laying bare the

devouring properties of European culture, which historically disallowed female (or any other) difference, but also criticising them. This would account for the demise of the twins' derivative works at the end of the scene 'desvaneceram-se, por inúteis' (faded away, being useless), while the high temple itself is prone to decay, withering into yellow leaves.

To what extent would it be possible, however, to interpret the scene differently and see the twin brothers as a caricature of the two Andrades, who happened to share the same surname although they were not related, and who had published the two monuments of Brazilian Modernism in 1928, the very same year as each other?[42] Admittedly, in real life, neither was fair or European-looking (in fact Mário was mixed race). But given that, following the ritualistic consumption of the blonde woman, Chapter VII concludes with the image of a carnivorous bird, projected onto the screen, it is tempting to wonder whether this might be an ironic self-representation of the author himself, aware of having cannibalised his Brazilian counterparts. If so, one could even go as far as to venture that Pedro may be here playfully 'consuming' the Brazilian *antropofagia* motto, provocatively enunciated by Oswald: 'Só a Antropofagia nos une' (Ruffinelli and Rocha 2000, 25) ('Only Anthropophagy unites us'). In fact, the haunting presence of the carnivorous bird effectively frames the entire chapter, since its close-up provides the motif for the illustration at the beginning, with its caption 'Pendia-lhe do bico uma pasta de sangue' ('A trickle of blood hung from its beak'). The lone bird's presence may moreover be seen to offer a reworking of the epilogue of *Macunaíma*, where the only memory that remained was that of a bird: a parrot, who lived to tell the entire tale to the author-narrator, before disappearing to Lisbon.[43]

On the other hand, it is true that ominous birds are a recurring motif in Pedro's paintings of the period. For instance, *Sentimento na planície* (*Feeling in the Plain*), a composition carried out during his stay in Brazil in 1941, shows a giant bird hovering in the sky, towering over a couple embracing.[44] It is also worth noting that the preceding chapter (VI) already featured a scene with a threatening bird, a raven (possibly a wry allusion to *The Raven* by Edgar Allen Poe): 'Com um pé apoiado em cada lado do meu corpo, estava um corvo preto enorme' ('An enormous black crow stood with a foot on either side of my body'). Rodrigues (2013) draws our attention to Pedro's cover illustration for a little-known 1942 book, *Correspondência frustrada*, by Carlos Tinoco, which depicts a human figure being devoured by a bird,[45] and convincingly reads it as a pictorial representation of the myth of Prometheus. He furthermore contends that this myth is also subliminally present in *Apenas uma narrativa*, not least bearing in mind the effect of the closing line of the novella, with its puzzling reference to the protagonist's liver (or lack thereof): 'Sei que viverei eternamente embora não tenha nem intestinos nem fígado' ('I know I will live for ever, even though I have neither entrails nor a liver'): indeed, according to Greek myth, Prometheus' liver was devoured by an eagle on a daily basis, yet regenerated itself overnight.

If we follow this line of interpretation, the uncanny scenario of Chapter VI, in which the protagonist's torture at the mercy of a raven in control of time seemed ongoing, may in fact have been superseded by the close of *Apenas uma narrativa*. Indeed, the protagonist's absence of liver may hint at the fact that he is at last freed from bodily shackles, putting a more positive complexion of the prospect of eternity. And, reading between the lines, this could be partly due to artistic redemption (Prometheus being also widely associated with artistic creativity), as we hope to now show in our next and final section.

4. Cyclical and Artistic Transformation

The novella closes with the certainty on the part of our ubiquitous narrator that he is endowed with both human characteristics, such as feelings (love of surprises), and divine ones, such as eternal life. As in Chapter I, there is a movement of ascension and fall. The material body, drunk and in transit, after a bath of moonlight, undergoes further metamorphoses and travel – colliding with a star and catching fire, before merging again into nature.

At this juncture, we cannot help but wonder whether this collision with a star is a parody of the last but one chapter of *Macunaíma*. Certainly at the close of both works, the protagonists travel back to their birthplace. However, one of the major differences between the Brazilian and the Portuguese characters resides in their respective final fates. Macunaíma ends up frozen as a lofty star in the sky 'solitário no vasto campo de céu' (1978, 145) ('solitary in the vast expense of sky'). As Madureira reminds us, the author of *Macunaíma* lamented, in a 1942 letter, its melancholic ending: 'everything in the last chapters was written in great agitation and sorrow… The two or three times I re-read that finale… I was overwhelmed by the same sadness, the same loving desire that it had not been so' (2005, 93). In this letter, Macunaíma's gloomy destiny is tellingly described by Andrade as a 'brilho *inútil*' ('*useless* shine'; italics in the original) and Madureira interprets this doom as 'a sort of spatialization of the lingering, genocidal silence repeated (or echoed) in the novel's epilogue' (p. 97). In *Apenas uma narrativa*, the star's eyes are coincidentally (in a fitting case of *hasard objectif*?) described as being 'inúteis na escuridão do céu' ('useless eyes in the darkness of the sky'). Tellingly, the collusion ignites the Portuguese protagonist and engenders his final transfiguration: the descent like rain into the Minho landscape, a figuration which can surely be viewed as heralding reintegration and potential reconciliation. A synthesis might be within grasp, then, through cosmic (and artistic) regeneration.

In that connection, it is worth emphasizing that, beneath the apparent chaos and open-endedness generated by multilayered uncanny, surrealist and antropophagic imagery, *Apenas uma narrativa* ultimately achieves some degree of legibility. A sense of balance prevails on a structural level, thanks to a fairly conventional story-telling format underlined by the neat division into ten chapters. The choice of ten is probably not a coincidence since this number typically signals the completion of a cycle, further underscored by the fact that the protagonist returns to his point of origin, Caminha. To that extent, Pedro's artistic preferences evidently extend beyond orthodox surrealist practice, for the reasons invoked in his afore mentioned 1941 interview: 'That which separates me most from the Surrealists is my willingness to accept Art as a fact, with all its resulting consequences: the control of intelligence over image association, the acceptance and study of conventional technical devices, in other words the outcome of pictorial culture'.[46]

With the benefit of hindsight, in terms of authorial control, what ultimately stands out as irrefutable evidence of Pedro's acceptance of 'Art as a fact, with all its resulting consequences' is his stunning reworking of the Mantegna's masterpiece, a conscious reworking that took pride of place in the cover illustration he produced for the first edition of *Apenas uma narrativa*.[47] It is finally reinstated, after over half a century of oblivion, in its rightful place – the cover to the present edition. This striking image presents a body lying horizontally. But, far from slavishly imitating his predecessor, Pedro operates a 180° turn, both literally and metaphorically: for now the scene depicts the body head first, with a perspective that expands into the landscape. In Pedro's modern recreation, then, the mutual interpenetration of man and nature adds a whole new dimension to Mantegna's original. The image conjures up a fresh set of associations insofar as, in contrast to the fifteenth century painting, it is dynamic and allows for an open-ended interpretation. It promotes at once death/defeat and birth/renewal, albeit a renewal suggestively predicated on a sense of ambiguity, for the illustration could either be seen in terms of a human being incorporated into the wider cosmos or conversely, of a body engendering nature.

As such, the merging together of body and landscape at the close of *Apenas uma narrativa* becomes retrospectively visually foreshadowed by its cover image. The convergence, enshrined *from the outset* in this visual representation, means that the story effectively encourages a cyclical understanding as opposed to a linear one.[48] Such *modus operandi* bears a strong resemblance to the more organic logic of dream-work. According to Freud in his *Interpretation of Dreams* 'A frequent device of dream distortion consists in presenting the final issue of the event or the conclusion of the train of thought at the beginning of the dream, and appending at the end of the dream the premises of the conclusion or the causes of the event' (1997, 210). In other words, one might argue that the cover image encapsulates, in a remarkable act of condensation, some of the undercurrents running through the novella, perhaps foreshadowing and furthering on some level its open-ended conclusion. It may, thus, function as a kind of pictorial *mise en abîme* of the entire text.

The fact that the picture is framed against a green background may be furthermore pregnant with meaning. In the broadest terms, green is the colour of nature, a fact which resonates with the overarching earth theme running through *Apenas uma narrativa*. More specifically for a Portuguese audience, however, green is also widely regarded as the colour of hope. In the context of a fictional world precariously balanced between the homely and the unhomely, and of a wider outside world ravaged by an ongoing World War II – seemingly devoid of God and traditional certainties – could this colour subliminally encode the tentative inscription of Pedro's perennial hope in the redemptive power of Art and artistic creativity?

Conclusion

As a cosmopolitan artist, Pedro sought to transform the landscape of twentieth century Portuguese prose fiction. This he achieved through the power of cultural cross-fertilization and productive synthesis. *Apenas uma narrativa* is certainly a *tour de force*, not least for the deftness with which it creatively incorporates and reworks some of the salient features of both Brazilian Modernism and French Surrealism into a single (and singular) text. As such, after Sá-Carneiro's pioneer 1914 *A Confissão de Lúcio*, it probably represents the most striking short narrative produced in Portugal in the first half of the last century. *Apenas uma narrativa*, then, far from being just a story (as Pedro himself teasingly chose to label it), might even be regarded as a tantalizing and visionary 'novel' (as he goes on to claim in his preface, facetiously stretching a point): a modernist miniature *bildungsroman*, teeming with irreverence, whose agenda simultaneously includes a questioning of the hegemonic premises of a dictatorship predicated on an ideology of 'God, Homeland, Family'.

Pedro went on to spend another extended period abroad, in 1944–1945, in wartime London, but he did not forget his 1942 masterpiece, as Rodrigues uncovers in the article that follows. Once back in Portugal, true to himself Pedro kept challenging the status quo and re-inventing himself as an artist for another two decades. Yet, right up to the end of his life, he continued to regard *Apenas uma narrativa* as his favourite book.[49] And with good reason, for it was on many levels his most imaginative and accomplished work.

Notes

1   For a recent examination of Salazar's regime in English, see Meneses (2009).

2   Reproductions of several of his paintings can be viewed online in *P: Portuguese Cultural Studies*, 5 (2013) <http://www2.let.uu.nl/solis/psc/p/volumefive.htm>. This issue, wholly devoted to different facets of Pedro's undertakings, includes an illustrated overview of his trajectory as a painter by José-Augusto França. The articles by Michele da Silva, Isabel Ponce de Leão and Bruno Silva Rodrigues also feature reproductions of Pedro's works.

3   For a recent introduction in English, see Castro (2009).

4   For a reproduction of the *Manifesto Antropófago*, and a range of scholarly analyses devoted to the antropophagic movement, see Ruffinelli and Rocha (2000).

5   For further details about Pedro and Cape Verde, see Semedo (1994, 23–31) and Oliveira (1998, xvi–xxi). According to Semedo, while Pedro's father was Portuguese, his mother was part Cape Verdean, part British (p. 24). His cultural links with Cape Verde were not as sustained as those he developed with other countries where he lived. Nonetheless, one decade later, in 1939, Pedro made a further journey to Africa, this time as a journalist, to cover a presidential trip to the then Portuguese colonies in a series of chronicles for *República* (10 Aug to 15 Sep 1939). His chronicle dated 28 July 1939 praises the *Claridade* movement, whose groundbreaking magazine had had its first three issues in 1936–7. (Crónicas da viagem a África do Presidente Óscar Carmona, in Pedro Archives E500-500-A-E).

6   For Pedro's abbreviated Portuguese translation of this manifesto, see Oliveira (1998, 95).

7   For comments on Pedro's pioneer role in the context of Portuguese Surrealism, see Marinho (1987, 22–26).

8   'Ressuscita a polémica entre novos e velhos', *Diário de Lisboa*, 20 April 1939, p. 5.

9   'António Pedro: exposição de pintura: catálogo', in Pedro Archives E5/594. The purchase of one of his paintings for the National Museum of Rio de Janeiro (*Nós dois no Brasil* [*The Two of Us in Brazil*]) was secured through the timely intervention of Carlos Drummond de Andrade, even though Pedro had yet to met him in person at that point in time, as his 'Autobiography' subsequently recalls (1979, 56).

10 For further details about the cultural weight of *Clima*, see Almeida (1976, 170–71). The

exhibition was held in Galeria Ita (or Edifício Ita), according to *Diário de S. Paulo* (see Andrade's article in Pedro Archives E5/637-639).

11   This preface was reproduced the following year in the first issue of Pedro's cultural magazine, *Variante* (1942).

12   October 1942 is mistakenly given as the date in his 'autobiography', where his recollection of dates is not always completely reliable. For further details about this exhibition, see Almeida (1976, 186–87).

13   There are three separate files of press cuttings relating to his Brazil. E5/637 (handwritten indication on the cover: Rio de Janeiro, Brasil, no. 1), E5/638 (handwritten indication on the cover: Rio de Janeiro, Brasil, no. 2) and E5/639 (handwritten indication on the cover São Paulo, Brasil, no. 3).

14   'A Arte Moderna em Portugal: meia hora com o pintor António Pedro', in Pedro Archives E5/637-639.

15   'O Português surrealista', in Pedro Achives E5/637-639. For his part, Almeida recounts a party (probably the same?), called 'Festa do mau-gosto' ('Party in Poor Taste') for which Pedro had challenged his guests to dress in the most tasteless way imaginable (1976, 171).

16   'António Pedro fala-nos do Brasil e dos brasileiros', in Pedro Archives E5/637-639. The article mentioned that Pedro had been back in his home country for one month already, which suggests an October return.

17   *Ibid.* Gilda was the niece of Mário de Andrade, about whom she went on to publish a monograph. Almeida explains that she subsequently became known by her married Mello e Souza (her husband was Antônio Cândido [Mello e Souza] and that Pedro did a painting of her, exhibited in São Paulo in 1941 (1976, 170). According to Antônio Cândido, this was 'um pequeno retrato a óleo representando Gilda de perfil' ('a small oil portrayal of Gilda's profile'), but it was subsequently lost (letter from Antônio Cândido to Cláudia Pazos Alonso, dated 26 Jun 2014).

18   'António Pedro fala-nos do Brasil e dos brasileiros', in Pedro Archives E5/637-639.

19   'Na exposição do pintor António Pedro', in Pedro Archives E5/637-639. See Antelo (2004) for a more detailed analysis.

20   Mário de Andrade's article, 'António Pedro', *Diário de S. Paulo*, 12 Aug 1941, can be found in Pedro Archives E5/639.

21   The picture, entitled *Bicho verde [Green animal]*, is dated 1940 and can be found in Mário de Andrade Archives, MA-0582.

22   In 1945, Antônio Cândido listed together 'o português António Pedro', Oswald de Andrade and Mário de Andrade, praising their rare attempts to 'estender o domínio do vocábulo sobre regiões mais complexas e mais inexprimíveis, ou fazer da ficção uma forma de conhecimento do mundo e das ideias', ('to extend language's realm into the most complex and inexpressible regions, or to turn fiction into a way of knowing the world and its ideas') in the context of a critical review of Lispector's debut novel ([1945] 1992, 97). In 1979, Fernando Azevedo considers that *Apenas uma narrativa* is 'próximo do Mário de Andrade de "Macunaíma", no antropofagismo da condição dela [da vida]' (1979, 40), but does not explore this insight further.

23   I owe this valuable information and several others contained in this article to Bruno Silva Rodrigues, to whom I wish to record my sincere thanks.

24   Ruffinelli and Rocha (2000) published a Portuguese translation of Picabia's 1920 *Manifeste Cannibale*, alongside the *Manifesto Antropófago*, (2000, 23–31).

25 Even when elsewhere Cândido associated Pedro with Surrealism, he continued to highlight the organizing role of the artist: 'o que há de extraordinário em certas obras surrrealistas [...] é a penetração da inteligência no meio do caos da associação livre ou da alusão, a fim de organizar a experiência intelectual e afetiva, comunicada pela obra. Assim são alguns contos de António Pedro' ('What is extraordinary in some surrealist works [...] is the penetration of intelligence amid the chaos of free association or allusion, so as to organise the intellectual and emotional experience communicated by the work. Some of António Pedro's short stories have this quality') ([1945] 1992, 106). It is curious to notice that Cândido continued to prefer the label of 'contos'.

26 'António Pedro: exposição de pintura: catálogo', with an intoduction by Jorge de Lima E5/594.

27 Ibid.

28 Ibid. 'feto' means both 'fern' and 'foetus' in Portuguese, a wordplay difficult to preserve in translation.

29 Garrett's novel was first published in 1843, and translated as Travels in My Homeland.

30 Mário de Andrade's article, in Pedro Archives E5/639.

31 'No S. P. N.: 7.ª Exposição de Arte Moderna', in Pedro Archives E5/640. The exhibition was inaugurated on 30 Dec 1942.

32 An earlier poem, 'Apostilha' [Note] dated March 1939, according to the manuscript version in Pedro Archives (see E5/538), also seems to prefigure thematically the characterization of Adam the planter, though it lacks any obvious biblical association. It begins 'O semeador tem feito todos os gestos / de semeador, / Lançando à terra aberta / Aquilo que traz e lhe chove em roda...', with the stanza ending 'Numa das leivas, o semeador/ Há-de-se um dia semear' ('The planter has been making all the gestures / of a planter, / throwing into the open earth / what he carries and drops like rain around him... / In one of the furrows, the planter / will one day plant himself'). 'Apostilha' formed part of a planned collection entitled Quando já nem se engana o coração com música, which remained unpublished. Even a cursory glance at this draft collection suggests thought-provoking links with Apenas uma narrativa. Oliveira, in his Antologia Poética, published selected poems from the manuscript, but not 'Apostilha' which he deemed unfinished (1998, 70). This is unlikely to be the case as 'Apostilha' was in fact published in Aventura (1943, 151–52).

33 The earliest reference to the book kept in the BNP files of press cuttings is dated February 1942 (announcing that the book would soon be released). See 'Notícia sobre o lançamento do livro do poeta futurista António Pedro', in Pedro Archives E5/640). Pedro's novella originally came out with Minerva, a publisher whose main retrospective claim to fame was that, five years later, it brought out Terra do pecado, the 1947 debut novel of Nobel laureate José Saramago.

34 To give but one example, the first edition of Esteiros by Soares Pereira, published one year before Apenas uma narrativa, featured illustrations by a young Álvaro Cunhal, who would go on to become the leader of the Portuguese Communist Party (Rothwell 2009, 159).

35 Most recently, the identification with Surrealism is documented by the fact that Chapter I, translated by Margaret Jull Costa, was published in an anthology of surrealist prose which includes extracts from several representative countries (Pedro, 1994).

36 'A Arte Moderna em Portugal: meia hora com o pintor António Pedro', in Pedro Archives E5/637-639.

37 The fact that he refers to himself as an anachronistic King must also be seen contextually, given the end of the Portuguese monarchy only a few years earlier in 1910. The sonnet, dated Paris 30 January 1916 (the year of Sá-Carneiro's suicide), first came to light posthumously in *Athena* in the 1920s. And only in 1937 did it become available in book-form, when it was published at the end of *Indícios de oiro*. Fernando Pessoa had also treated the theme of a deposed King in 'Abdicação', an extraordinary sonnet dating from 1913, which concludes with a return into the landscape. For an English translation of the latter, please see Pessoa (2006, 278).

38 The translation into English is my own. For a plot summary, please see Rosenberg (2006, 81–83).

39 The *Manifesto Antropófago* featured a reproduction of *Aboporu*. For a recent discussion of the significance of this manifesto in a Latin American context, see Rosenberg (2006).

40 Although António Pedro's family on his father's side originated from Moledo, next door to Caminha, Pedro himself was in fact born in Cape Verde, as previously mentioned. Accordingly, on a personal level, Caminha may indirectly come to stand for the constructed nature of origins. It is perhaps also worth noting that, as a surname, in a fitting case of *hasard objectif*, Caminha is linked to another foundational myth of origin: the 'discovery' of Brazil recounted in the *Carta* by Pero Vaz de Caminha, whose formal style was parodied in *Macunaima's* 'Carta pras Icamiabas'.

41 Incidentally, in the context of Brazilian Modernism, human deformation was used by Tarsila as a defamiliarizing device in her *Abaporu*, who famously featured a disproportionately small head compared to the rest of its body.

42 Furthermore, the charge of effeminacy, which was levelled at Mário by Oswald, and led to their estrangement, might have been magnified here to produce the caricatural image of homosexual siblings.

43 The parrot's transatlantic flight is perhaps loosely mirrored in reverse by the Portuguese's protagonist's oneiric transposition to Mexico in the chapter that follows.

44 In the earlier painting 'O Quarto alugado' ('The Rented Room') (1940), a scary figure, half bird and half-man, held its female prey. For a reproduction of this image, please see Rocha (2013, 25).

45 Tinoco's work came out in 1942, the very same year as *Apenas uma narrativa*. For a reproduction of its book-cover see Rodrigues (2013, 63).

46 'A Arte Moderna em Portugal: meia hora com o pintor António Pedro', in Pedro Archives E5/637-639.

47 The fact that this intertextuality was deliberate is attested by the existence of another slightly different design for the cover of *Apenas uma narrativa* (featured in *1.ᵃ Exposição dos artistas ilustradores modernos*, held in Lisbon and Porto in April–May 1942). See Appendix 4 for a reproduction of this image, more obviously in dialogue with Mantegna in the detail of the feet, no longer present in the final version.

48 It is worth noting that, in terms of individual chapters, this strategy is also deployed twice, in Chapters I and VII, where each of the captions and its respective illustration is taken from the close of the chapter in question. The case of Chapter VII is especially striking, because the protagonist declares in his opening sentence: 'era tão verdade que ainda não tinha acontecido' ('it was so true that it hadn't yet happened'). These disturbing cover images, likewise, are so 'true' that the stories they tell have not yet happened when we first

see them. By the second encounter with the caption statement, however, the reader is likely to experience subconsciously an uncanny sense of *déjà vu*.

49 In a letter sent to Aquilino Ribeiro, postmarked 11 Mar 1963, Pedro stated 'Dediquei-lhe o meu livro de que mais gosto – se é que gosto de algum' ('Of my books, I dedicated to you the one I like best – insofar I like any of them'). See Aquilino Ribeiro Archives D11/5190-5191).

Bibliography

Primary Sources
António P. *Apenas uma narrativa* (Lisbon: Minerva, 1942).
António P. '3 poemas', *Aventura*, Jul 1943, pp. 151–52.
António P. 'Autobiografia', in *António Pedro 1909–1966* (Lisbon: Fundação Calouste Gulbenkian, 1979), pp. 54–58.
António P. Chapter I of 'Just a Story' in *The Dedalus Book of Surrealism*, ed. M. Richardson, trans. M. J. Costa, 2 vols (Sawtry: Dedalus, 1994), II: *The Myth of the World*, pp. 59–61.
António P. 'Motim: conto irracional', *Juventude*, Dec 1939, p. 21.

António Pedro Archives, Biblioteca Nacional de Portugal, Lisbon
'Crónicas da viagem a África do Presidente Óscar Carmona', E500-500-A-E.
'Quando já nem se engana o coração com música: poemas', E5/538.
'António Pedro: exposição de pintura: catálogo', with an intoduction by Jorge de Lima, E5/594.
Press cuttings, 1941, E5/637–639:
    Andrade, M. de, 'António Pedro', *Diário de S. Paulo*, 12 Aug 1941.
    'António Pedro fala-nos do Brasil e dos brasileiros', *Acção*, 6 Nov 1941.
    'A Arte Moderna em Portugal: meia hora com o pintor António Pedro', *Dom Casmurro*, 19 Apr 1941.
    'Na exposição do pintor António Pedro', *O Dia*, 6 Aug 1941.
    Pedro, António, 'Última folha de um diário de viagem: De António Pedro ao Jorge de Lima', *Dom Casmurro*, 26 Apr 1941.
    'O Português surrealista', *Planalto*, 15 Aug 1941.
Press cuttings, 1941–1943, E5/640:
    'Notícia sobre o lançamento do livro do poeta futurista António Pedro', *O Figueirense*, 21 Feb 1942.
    'No S. P. N.: 7.ª Exposição de Arte Moderna', *Seara Nova*, 23 Jan 1943.

Aquilino Ribeiro Archives, Biblioteca Nacional de Portugal, Lisbon
Cartas de António Pedro para Aquilino Ribeiro, D11/5190-5191.

Mário de Andrade Archives, Instituto Estudos Brasileiros, São Paulo, Brasil
Carta anterior a 22 Outubro 1941 de António Pedro para Mário de Andrade,
    MA-C-CPL5646.
Carta datada de 22 Outubro 1941 de António Pedro para Mário de Andrade,
    MA-C-CPL5647.
Bilhete sem data de António Pedro para Mário de Andrade, MA-C-CPL5648.
'Bicho verde', MA-0582.

Secondary Sources
Alçada, J. N. 'Apenas uma narrativa de António Pedro, ou o romance surrealista em
    Portugal', *Revista da Biblioteca Nacional*, 2 (1982), 85–100.
Almeida, P. M. de *De Anita ao Museu* (São Paulo: Perspectiva, 1976).
Andrade, M. de *Macunaíma: o herói sem nenhum caráter*. ed. T. P. Ancona Lopez (São
    Paulo: Secretaria da Cultura, Ciência e Tecnologia, 1978).
Andrade, M. de *Macunaíma*, trans. E. A. Goodland (London: Quartet, 1984).
Antelo, R. 'Antonio Pedro e a condição acefálica', *Semear*, 9 (2004), 161–94.
'Os Artistas ilustradores modernos no S. P. N.', *Panorama*, Jun 1942, p. 17.
Azevedo, F. 'O Ensaísta' in *António Pedro 1909–1966* (Lisbon: Fundação Calouste
    Gulbenkian, 1979), pp. 38–40.
Bhabha, H. *Nation and Narration* (London: Routledge, 1990).
Breton, A. *Manifestoes of Surrealism*, trans. H. R. Lane and R. Seaver (Ann Arbor:
    University of Michigan Press, 1972).
Breton, A. *Œuvres complètes* (Paris: Gallimard, 1988), 4 vols.
Breton, A. *Nadja*, trans. H. Richard (London: Penguin, 1999).
Cândido, A. 'Surrealismo no Brasil', in *Brigada ligeira e outros escritos*, [1945] (São
    Paulo: UNESP, 1992).
Cândido, A. 'Intercâmbio e António Pedro', *Clima*, July 1941, pp. 60–61.
Cândido, A. '[Recensão a *Apenas uma narrativa*]', *Clima*, July 1942, pp. 88–91.
Castro, M. G. de 'Fernando Pessoa and Modernism', in *A Companion to Portuguese
    Literature*, ed. S. Parkinson, C. Pazos-Alonso and T. F. Earle (Woodbridge: Tamesis,
    2009), pp. 144–56.
França, J.-A. 'António Pedro and António Dacosta', *Colóquio: Revista de artes e letras*,
    32 (1965), 26–32.
França, J.-A. 'Deux romans insolites, "Nome de Guerra" d'Almada Negreiros et "Apenas
    uma narrativa" d'António Pedro', in *Actes du colloque l'enseignement et l'expansion
    de la littérature portugaise en France* (Paris: Fond. Calouste Gulbenkian – Centre
    Culturel Portugais, 1986), pp. 159–165.
Freud, S. *The Interpretation of Dreams*, trans. A. A. Brill (Ware: Wordsworth, 1997).
Freud, S. *The Uncanny*, ed. D. McLintock, trans. H. Haughton (London: Penguin,
    2003).
Madureira L. *Cannibal Modernities. Postcoloniality and the Avant-Garde in Caribbean*

and Brazilian Literature (Charlottesville and London: University of Virginia Press, 2005).

Margarido, A. 'Les imaginaires multiples de António Pedro', *Arquivos do Centro Cultural Português*, XXV (1988), pp. 5–69.

Marinho, M. de F. *O Surrealismo em Portugal* (Lisbon: Imprensa Nacional-Casa da Moeda, 1987).

Meneses, F. R. de *Salazar: A Political Biography* (New York: Enigma Books 2009).

Oliveira, F. M. Introduction to *Antologia Poética* (Braga: Angelus Novus, 1998).

Pazos A. and B. Silva Rodrigues (eds) 'A Man of Many (P)arts', *P: Portuguese Cultural Studies*, 5 (2013), issue devoted to António Pedro, <http://www2.let.uu.nl/solis/psc/p/volumefive.htm>.

Pessoa, F. *A Little Larger Than The Entire Universe*, trans. R. Zenith (London: Penguin, 2006).

'Ressuscita a polémica entre novos e velhos', *Diário de Lisboa*, 20 April 1939, p. 5.

Rocha, M. 'A Tensão para o inanimado ou a "emergência da morte na vida" nas mulheres-árvore de António Pedro', *P: Portuguese Cultural Studies*, 5 (2013), 17–31, <www2.let.uu.nl/solis/psc/p/pvolumefivepapers/p5rocha.pdf>.

Rodrigues, B. S. 'Estratégias de Deformação e Transformação em *Apenas uma narrativa*', *P: Portuguese Cultural Studies*, 5 (2013), 46–69, <www2.let.uu.nl/solis/psc/p/pvolumefivepapers/p5silvarodrigues.pdf>.

Rodrigues, B. S. 'O Surrealismo e as relações entre a Literatura e a Pintura em *Apenas uma narrativa* de António Pedro', unpublished Masters thesis, University of Oxford, 2010.

Rosenberg, F. *The Avant-Garde and Geopolitics in Latin America*, (Pittsburgh: University of Pittsburgh Press, 2006).

Rothwell, P. 'Narrative and Drama during the Dictatorship', in *A Companion to Portuguese Literature*, ed. S. Parkinson, C. Pazos-Alonso and T. F. Earle (Woodbridge: Tamesis, 2009), pp. 157–67.

Ruffinelli, J. and J. C. de Castro Rocha, 'Antropofagia Hoje?', Special issue of *Nuevo Texto Crítico* (2000). Revised and expanded as *Antropofagia Hoje? Oswald de Andrade em cena* (São Paulo: É Realizações Editora, 2011).

Sá-Carneiro, M. de *Poemas Completos* (Lisbon: Assírio and Alvim, 1996).

Sá-Carneiro, M. de *Lúcio's Confession*, trans. M. Jull Costa (Swatry: Dedalus, 1993).

Semedo, M. B. 'António Pedro: uma influência na sombra', in *Caboverdianamente Ensaiando* (São Vicente: Ilheu Editora, 1994), vol 1, pp. 23–31.

Ungaretti, G. 'Prefácio da exposição de A. Pedro em S.Paulo', *Variante*, (1942), pp. 65–72.

Filmography
Macunaíma: Joaquim Pedro de Andrade (1969).

ANTÓNIO PEDRO IN BRITAIN
AND THE LONDON SURREALISTS (1944–1945)

In the midst of global conflict, António Pedro left for London to join some of his countrymen employed by the Portuguese section of the BBC. Almost seventy years have passed since then and it is now possible, with the help of a few letters[1] not previously considered under the perspective of Pedro's stay in England, to follow and understand in greater detail his participation in the group of surrealists in London and the partial publication of *Apenas uma narrativa* in English. The range of experiences that Pedro accumulated during his time in Britain constituted one of the most enriching moments of his multidisciplinary journey and would inspire the activities he undertook on his return to Portugal. It was a moment in his life which, as Pedro himself would affirm, was 'indispensável à minha experiência de habitante deste mundo' ['indispensable to my experience as citizen of this world'].[2]

1. The time at the BBC and the gestation of new projects

The departure took place in early January 1944. In his luggage, Pedro carried a six-month contract (5 January to 5 July 1944) as translator and broadcaster, which would eventually be extended until almost the end of 1945, when he returned to Portugal. He also carried the exploratory instinct which characterised him, in this case an eagerness to observe, to participate *in loco* and to transmit to others the means of resistance put into effect in the last European bastion against Nazi ambition. Already a few years earlier, according to his autobiography, he ended his visit to Brazil boarding what he thought would be the last ship to Portugal before it was invaded (which evidently never came to pass) (Pedro 1979, 54). Beyond revealing a wish to return to his family and the country where he grew up, this gesture likewise suggests a desire to experience the unfolding of the war at the heart of the action. As one BBC director would later recall 'he came to this country with every desire to be of assistance to Britain's War Efforts'.[3] Who knows if the impulse which drew him to London, a city already devastated by aerial bombardment and living under its constant threat, did not stem also from the Scottish-Irish roots he inherited from his maternal grandmother, whom he believed to be a niece of the English Romantic poet Walter Savage Landor, although this is unlikely.

For almost two years, Pedro translated and produced radio programmes. As time went on and his use of the microphone improved, he captivated audiences making 'a real impact on Portuguese listeners' and himself indispensable to the Portuguese section of the BBC. This was recognised by the Corporation itself in April 1945, in reaction to Pedro's first letter of resignation, later retracted: 'his loss at the present time would obviously be serious for us'.[4] In fact, Pedro's relationship with the BBC had its lows as well as highs, particularly from 1945 onwards, whether due to practical factors (the Corporation's delay in appointing a new announcer and a typist left him for a while overloaded with work), or to its strategic and political orientation. The latter would decisively affect Pedro's motivation, limiting the room he had to work in and the dynamism of his *Crónicas de segunda-feira* (*Monday Chronicles*), which he thought were 'his only worthwhile contribution of the week and that the rest of the work he was asked to do in the Section he looked upon as useless'.[5] Pedro's *Crónicas* recounted life in the British Isles, and inevitably the war, and were broadcast almost continuously every week from 17 January 1944 to 15 October 1945. He even considered publishing a selection of these chronicles along with other radio addresses and prepared a manuscript with this purpose in mind, having sought the requisite authorisation from the Corporation.[6] However, the BBC directors prevented the publication by raising various concerns, in a process which exposes the political forces that affected the Corporation's independence. In fact, in order to avoid direct insults to the Salazar regime and in line with the complex system which governed the relationship between the two countries, editorial content and the free expression of the Portuguese broadcasters were subject to regulation. Accordingly, some of the chronicles produced by Pedro, especially those which contained the most explicit comments in favour of democracy, were censored (Ribeiro 2010; 2013).

Yet Pedro remained one of the most rebellious radio-soldiers, frequently ignoring instructions from above and using his broadcasts to make political comments, albeit often more obliquely. Such behaviour made him a thorn in the side of the political powers-that-be in Portugal. One such example is the reading of the poem 'Europa' by Adolfo Casais Monteiro, which possessed a clear message on freedom.[7] According to various contemporary sources, Pedro's chronicles provided a place for meeting and reflection like no other (França 1979, 44). The BBC thus had at its disposal a representative of undeniable value to consolidate amongst the Portuguese the image of commitment to truth which it had been creating, and the Portuguese audiences corresponded by listening in massive numbers to its broadcasts. As Nelson Ribeiro highlights, the BBC represented a significant weapon against Nazi propaganda in Portugal (Ribeiro 2010). For Pedro this was an opportunity to spread a rare wave of freedom through the environment of censorship which Portugal then routinely experienced. In this way, the fame of the BBC would also have been an important impetus for his departure, since the perspective of 'fighting' for liberty represented possibly a moment of personal atonement for the political position he had taken in the 1930s, in favour of anti-parliamentary National-Syndicalism. The experience on the radio was thus the first reward of his relocation, inspirational to the extent that he would subsequently propose programmes for Portuguese radio, although to little avail, which is not surprising given the close surveillance of the regime over Pedro's movements on his return to Portugal.

Still connected to the BBC, Pedro was involved in a small radio theatre group on the London Transcription Service. This was a rather important experience as it provided contact with the reality of British theatre. It no doubt reinforced his interest in drama which dated back to his adolescence in La Guardia, when he participated in dozens of school plays. As a consequence, immediately upon his return to Portugal, Pedro would conceive an alternative theatre company by the name of *Pátio das comédias*,[8] although it was only from the 1950s onwards that he would embark on activities as a dramatist, playwriter and theatre director. His work contributed to the renewal of Portuguese theatre, a renewal which, thus, was in part built upon his experience in England.

England also contributed to Pedro's ambition, inspired by the *Evening Standard*, to create a new evening newspaper of large circulation for Lisbon. He put forward this idea in a letter from London in July 1945, to some friends in Portugal, and he sought to implement it after his return, hoping for an improvement in press freedom. The editorial line envisaged for this newspaper reflected Pedro's cosmopolitan spirit, heightened by his British sojourn: 'esse Jornal, de carácter francamente liberal e progressivo, manter-se-á independente de qualquer filiação partidária, e terá como objectivo principal "europeizar" Portugal, desprovincializar Lisboa e valorizar as expressões nacionais que personalizam o país no concerto das nações europeias' ('this newspaper, frankly liberal and progressive in character, will remain free from affiliation to any political party, and its main objective will be to 'europeanise' Portugal, de-provincialise Lisbon and to emphasize the national singularities which single out the country amongst European nations').[9] Pedro was trying to save Portugal from its inward-looking condition, in a bid to offer his country the artistic and social developments taking place in northern Europe, a desire he had already put into practice, although fleetingly, one decade earlier when he returned from his stay in Paris (1934–1935), through the publication of a column entitled '*Climat parisien*', described as a '*feuille internationale d'art moderne paraissant toutes les quinzaines*' ('international page on modern art, published every fortnight') in *Fradique* and *Revelação* (December 1935 and January 1936 respectively).

Multiple other activities can be related to his stay in England: firstly, the outline for a book about London with the title *Londres, por António Pedro*, a manuscript now in his archive which shows a Pedro who scrutinises the routines of the city and its inhabitants;[10] secondly, the translation with José Marinho of the *The Prince and the Pauper* by Mark Twain, published in Lisbon in April 1945 by Inquérito.[11] Thirdly, he took part, alongside other members of the international team at the BBC, in a question and answer session which took place in the early months of 1944 at the Student Association of the University of Birmingham (Pedro would later recall answering a question posed by a sixteen-year-old girl who asked him to describe a city illuminated at night, given that Lisbon, unlike London, did not enforce a black-out).[12] Furthermore, his contact with film-maker Alberto Cavalcanti can be traced to this period. Pedro invited Cavalcanti to direct a film based on the cinematic script *As Casas da areia* or *Argil*, co-written by Pedro himself and Dr. Rosenfield around 1947 which the Italian accepted. Mainly due to financial reasons, the film was never produced (França 1990, 130–31).

Finally, within months of his arrival, Pedro's attraction to artistic avant-garde movements led to the composition of some surrealist poems, dated May 1944, such as 'Sinagoga', 'Devia haver livros de racionamento mesmo para o entusiasmo (único poema de guerra)' and 'Four Little Portuguese Poems', the latter displaying affinities with the style and themes of *Apenas uma narrativa*.[13] It is also known that he was invited to contribute with occasional articles to *Horizon: a Review of Literature and Art* (1940–1950), in which a number of surrealists collaborated, as well as other artists and writers of note,[14] and to give a lecture at the Caravela Club on modern Brazilian art (although it is not known for certain whether he delivered it). These happened between October and December 1944, according to the permission he sought from the BBC, which was granted. In the case of *Horizon*, Pedro mentioned in his request that he was 'engaged upon writing an article on Portugal'.[15]

2. Pedro's involvement with the London 'philo-surrealists'

Alongside these numerous activities, Pedro's participation in the projects of the London surrealists is especially noteworthy. Two factors brought about his involvement: the acquaintance and affinity which he possessed with Surrealism, at least since his Paris days; and the fact that some members of the group also worked at the BBC, as was the case of Feyyaz Fergar and especially those who would become central figures of the group: Edouard Léon Théodore Mesens and Jacques-Bernard Brunius. This surrealist group represented the continuation of the English Surrealist Group, begun in 1936, which had almost completely disintegrated by 1940 due to the war (Agar). However, some members of the original group continued, in the meantime, to organise meetings with some regularity, now in the café-cum-restaurant Barcelona in Soho, now in the houses of Roland Penrose or Mesens, in Hampstead, or even, according to Pedro himself, sometimes in the 'Restaurante Chinês' or the 'Clube Português'.[16] These get-togethers 'consisted of a lot of drink, dinner, surrealist games ("exquisite corpse" and collective picture), and recitations of poetry', as well as discussion of current affairs (Ray, 252).[17]

Notwithstanding this creative and intellectual health, the group was above all a conglomeration of surrealist enthusiasts, to different degrees and with different objectives, and was therefore far from constituting a cohesive orchestra conducted by a single baton. Its unstable leadership, the lack of rigour in its selection of new members and the deficiency in its promotion of collective discussion which might help to refine an ideological position and a strategy of actions common to all, meant that heterogeneity prevailed in the group and little collective work was produced. This instability continued throughout 1944 as a result of a number of spats between its members. In a letter sent to Mesens on 23 February 1945 by Brunius himself, the nature of the 'pseudo-groupe' was called into question: 'je ne pouvais en aucune façon considérer ce groupe comme surréaliste, ni même comme un groupe homogène. Je maintiens depuis des mois qu'il s'agit tout au plus d'un groupe d'amis ou [*sic*] les divergences sont assez négligeables pour qu'on puisse parler de choses et d'autres sans se dégoûter les uns des autres, mais où les divergences sont trop importantes pour qu'on puisse envisager une *activité* commune' ('I could not consider, in any way, this group as surrealist or even as a homogeneous group. I have been defending for months that it is a group of friends at best where the divergences are negligible enough to allow the discussion of various subjects without putting anyone off, but where those divergences are much too important to envisage a common *activity*').[18]

Several sources confirm Pedro's participation in the group meetings. Although it is not known precisely when it began and ended, it must have been during 1945. It is quite likely that some collaboration existed already in 1944, the date which Patrick Waldberg, one of the attendees, gives as the moment when 'António nous apparut à Londres' ('António appeared to us in London') (p. 399). Apart from the aforementioned letter from Brunius which includes Pedro as one of the member of the group in February 1945, Michael Remy also lists Pedro as a participant in at least one out of two important meetings in 1945. At the first of these, on 30 August, the possible means for shaping unity and formalizing the group would have been explored. The implementation of a monthly subscription and the reactivation of the name 'Surrealist Group in England' were also discussed. The second meeting took place on 12 September, with Pedro on the list of participants. Here the group would have decided to organise public debates and exhibitions (Remy, 280–81). George Melly, for his part, referring to the first meeting he attended, which took place in the restaurant Barcelona, counts Pedro amongst those present and although a specific date is not given, it is likely to have been towards the end of 1945 (p. 11; Remy, 275).

According to assertions made by Brunius in the aforementioned letter, the recruitment of Pedro did not follow the usual pattern by which some members joined the group, based on approval without criteria, without a waiting period, as a result of a harried Mesens, leading to the inclusion of people whose relationship with Surrealism was dubious or inconsistent. On the contrary, Pedro's recruitment was the full responsibility of Brunius and only took place after a number of meetings over several months, ending in the Frenchman's acceptance of Pedro 'avec la certitude qu'il était de tous ceux que nous avions rencontré celui avec lequel nous avions le plus de points communs' ('with the assurance that he was, of all those we had encountered, the one with whom we had more points in common').[19] In his reply, Mesens agrees with this view and supplies his own: 'Je t'accorde que Pedro vaut mieux que d'autres. Mais pourquoi? Parce qu'il est *plus âgé*, qu'il a *plus d'expérience humain* [*sic*] et l'habitude d'un certain commerce mondain' ('I agree with you that Pedro is better than others. But why? Because he is *older*, because he *has more human experience* and he is used to a fair amount of worldly dealings').[20] To these personal characteristics can be added those identified in Pedro by Patrick Waldberg: a 'dandysme d'allure et de langage' ('Dandy in appearance and language') linked to an 'inquiétude ontologique' ('ontological disquiet') (p. 399). However, defending himself against the accusation of carelessness which Brunius levelled against him and giving Pedro's recruitment as an example, Mesens attacks the certainty displayed by his colleague regarding the Portuguese man's qualities: 'Pedro m'a avoué sans détours, et sans que je lui pose de question, qu'il fût <u>fasciste</u> et futuriste à une époque de sa vie' ('Pedro confessed to me without skirting around the issue, and without any probing on my part, that he had been a *fascist* and a futurist once upon a time').[21] This statement is interesting for two reasons. On the one hand, it reveals that Pedro did not hide the period, as previously mentioned, especially between 1931 and 1933, when he actively defended for Portugal the anti-parliamentary, anti-liberal, anti-middle-class political system, which had substituted the Military Dictatorship installed in 1926 after the sixteen chaotic years of the first Republic. On the other hand, if one bears in mind that National-Syndicalism split at the end of 1933 into one faction which followed the regime and another which opposed it (the latter withdrew to the shadows where it would draw in Pedro), this confession confirms the anti-regime stance which he henceforth adopted. His anti-Salazar position was, therefore, clear amongst the members of the London surrealists.[22]

The artistic and cultural baggage which Pedro brought from Portugal constituted thus important points in his favour, facilitating his integration in the group but also the development of privileged relationships with Patrick Waldberg, Brunius, and in particular with Mesens, whose friendship went beyond the 'simples conhecimento ocasional' ('simple casual acquaintance'), as Pedro would later remember (1979, 56). Mesens and Pedro were indeed both writers as well as visual artists. Like Mesens, who was director of the London Gallery, Pedro had founded a modern art gallery in Lisbon, the UP (1933), through which he sponsored and organised avant-garde exhibitions, including Vieira da Silva's first show in the capital (1935). Painting was likewise an important aspect of Pedro's profile when he arrived in England. The reproduction of one of his paintings in *Free Unions/Unions Libres* (1946) was not accidental nor was the fact that some members of the group remember him as 'a Portuguese painter' (Melly, 11). It is therefore not surprising that Pedro came to organise an exhibition together with Mesens and, moreover, that works of his featured in at least five others. The first, titled *Surrealist Diversity: 1915–1945*, was open to the public in The Arcade Gallery (28 Old Bond St) between 4 and 30 October 1945 and displayed work by twenty-one artists displaced by war, including Jean Arp, De Chirico, Delvaux, Ernst, Giacometti, Klee, Magritte, Miró, Picasso, Man Ray and Pedro himself, represented by the painting *Pássaro de mãos* (1944), which seems to have disappeared.[23]

The other five all took place in The London Gallery (23 Brook St), reopened by Mesens in 1946, in other words after Pedro had returned to Portugal. Since the invitations for these exhibitions included Pedro's name in the list of participating artists, it can be assumed that at least one of his works was on display. The exhibitions were: one to mark the reopening of the gallery on 5 November 1946; another open to the public between 10 December 1946 and 11 January 1947 titled *New Year Old Names New Age New Names No Christmas Imagery New World* which included works by Ernst, Kandisky, Magritte, Picasso, Miró, Scottie Wilson, Arp, Hubert, amongst others; in October 1947 the exhibition presented in tandem with another titled *The Temptation of St Anthony* with John Craxton, Lucian Freud, Jesus Reis and Scottie Wilson; and finally, *New York by New Names for the New Year*, an exhibition which ran between December 1947 and January 1948 with works by Lucien Freud, Klee, Gris, Léger, Masson, Picasso, Chagall, Miró, Ernst, Magritte, Arp, *etc.*[24] Although it is not known which works by Pedro were included on these occasions, on 26 April 1972 seven paintings by Pedro were sold by Sotheby's in London.[25] These paintings came from Mesens' estate, which consequently makes it probable that they were the ones that had featured in the exhibitions. As the majority of them are dated from 1944–45, it is quite likely that Pedro had produced them in England, where they were later acquired by Mesens.[26] Only *A Fantastic Figure and Animal in a Interior* (1944) and *Interior with Skeleton* (1944) have been made public so far, although it is possible to access a reproduction of *Nude Woman* (1945) (Appendix 5) in the sale catalogue.[27]

Beyond these works, Pedro would have shown his surrealist colleagues some of his earlier ones, albeit as reproductions taken from catalogues or magazines, for instance possibly the three paintings which Patrick Waldberg would reproduce in his *Les Demeures d'Hypnos* (1976) (pp. 398, 400–01)[28] and the canvas to which Serge Senninger refers: 'J'avais aimé de lui [Pedro] un tableau qui représentait un visage féminin où les yeux étaient remplacés par des lèvres (avec rouge à lèvres) et la bouche par un oeil *cyclopéen*' ('I had rather liked a painting of his [Pedro] which represented a female face where the eyes had been replaced by lips (with lipstick) and a mouth by a *Cyclopean* eye').[29] It is possible that Serge Senninger saw this figure in one of Pedro's 'London' paintings yet to be identified, but the theme already appeared in the second panel of the *Tríptico solto de Moledo* (1943), which seems to be itself a variation on the famous *Le Viol* (1934) by Magritte or *Composition With Portrait* (1935) by Victor Brauner.

Recognised, then, as an experienced figure boasting a solid background in Surrealism, Pedro came to assume an important role in the group dynamic, above all with regard to editorial projects. This is not surprising, since he had extensive experience in this field. It is again Brunius who writes: 'Quant aux possibilités d'action une fois les positions clarifiées, elles restent pour l'instant faibles. Les principales sont liées aux publications possibles et résident surtout entre tes [Mesens] mains et celles de Pedro' ('Regarding possibilities for action, once clarified the positions, they remain weak for now. The main ones are linked to potential publications and they reside mainly in your hands and Pedro's').[30] In fact, Pedro would propose a publication along the lines of an encyclopaedia for which he hoped to secure contributors from abroad. Brunius refers to this project as *ABC* and suggests that it be discussed in a meeting as an example of an individual idea put to the service of the group. However, the *ABC* project was never completed by the London group, as Brunius states in January 1946, almost one year after his first reference to the subject: 'La revue en forme de petit ABC de l'Encyclopédie est pour l'instant abandonnée. Nous n'étions pas assez nombreux pour la faire sans matériel venu d'ailleurs. António Pedro qui devait la faire est reparti au Portugal' ('The publication in the form of a small Encyclopedia ABC is for now abandoned. We were not sufficient in numbers to carry it out without material from abroad. António Pedro, who should have produced it, has returned to Portugal').[31] However, the *ABC* would be later reformulated by Patrick Waldberg with the help of other French surrealists as *Le Da Costa Encyclopédique*. Simon Watson Taylor himself suggests it: 'as JB's [Brunius] letter makes clear, it was indeed António Pedro Da Costa who initiated the idea, along with his old pal Waldberg (and W.'s pal Duchamp). Jacques' [Brunius] "ABC" refers to the Da Costa, which maybe hadn't yet received that title.' He further adds that 'The D. C. [Da Costa] Encyclopédique had nothing to do with the English surrealist group (or "pseudo-group", as Jacques neatly designates it), except that Patrick and Pedro were living in London at the time'.[32]

Pedro was not, however, part of this re-configuration, as is revealed by the contents of a letter he received from Patrick Waldberg himself:

> J'ai mis sur pied, avec quelques amis, la publication prochaine du 'Grand da Costa Encyclopédique', une œuvre de remise en question de toutes les données acquises, et en particulier de tous les mots. Se présentant dans la forme d'un 'Larousse Mensuel', le da Costa, qui commence à la lettre E et au fascicule 2 prétend apporter des changements profonds à l'usage de la parole et de l'écriture. Il va de soi que ta collaboration serait précieuse.

> (With the help of some friends, I came up with the publication of the forthcoming 'Great Encyclopedia Da Costa', a work which questions all acquired data and

in particular all words. Presenting itself as a monthly Larousse, the Da Costa, which begins with the letter E and on the second instalment, intends to bring profound changes in the use of speech and writing. It goes without saying that your contribution would be priceless).[33]

Patrick does not directly imply Pedro in the origin of the encyclopedia nor mentions the aborted *ABC*. This suggests, as Kleiber defends, that the background for the idea may have been built before Pedro's appearance in London (p. 113). It is however clear that a direct link can be established between the two projects. The first volume of this encyclopedia, deliberately headless and anonymous, appeared in October 1947 in some bookshops in Saint-Germain-des-Prés, Paris. Its preparation occupied at least the second half of 1946, during which time it was mentioned in letters between Isabelle and Patrick Waldberg and also in the December edition of *London Gallery News* (an informative bulletin of Mesens' gallery): 'Da Costa to publish his encyclopaedia' (Waldberg, M., 435; Brotchie, *Encyclopaedia*, 17). The volume for sale in Parisian bookshops pretended the collection was already well advanced, as it was the seventh issue of volume II. This parody is confirmed by its contents, since the definitions it contained (composed of original texts or citations of works with surrealist leanings) do not begin with the letter A, but the letter E. Moreover, the initial text began part way through a word. This 'first' instalment was followed by two other issues in 1948 and 1949, numbered I and II, this time identifying its editors and contributors, and with a slightly revised title: *Le Memento Universel Da Costa*. It is now known that the Da Costa publications were organised by Robert Lebel and Isabelle Waldberg, with the collaboration of Duchamp and using material which Patrick Waldberg had collected during the war or shortly after it ended. The authorship of some of the direct collaborative texts present in the first anonymous volume is also known, thanks to the existence of a copy annotated by Patrick Waldberg himself. It includes such names as: Breton, Brunius, Bataille, Lebel and Duchamp (Brotchie, *Encyclopaedia*, 18).[34]

    It is unlikely that Pedro contributed to any of the *Da Costa* publications despite Patrick's invitation. It is worth mentioning nevertheless that, following his return in Portugal, he would start his own encyclopaedic project, named *Dicionário prático ilustrado*, although he never completed it. It contained several entries in English, all under the letter A, which suggests that these could have originally been designed to form part of the *ABC* or even a later volume of *Le Memento Universel Da Costa*.[35]

    At this point I ought, perhaps, to clarify the origin of the epithet 'Da Costa', related to the surname of António Pedro (da Costa). Its use and later dissemination are owed to an event which took place at the heart of the London surrealist group. Serge Senninger recounts that, at the beginning of one of the group meetings, which happened somewhere between the end of 1944 and the beginning of 1945, Brunius or Mesens greeted Pedro by his surname and continued, in jest, to greet the rest of those present in the same fashion, christening them all Da Costa. Pedro supposedly then commented that the gesture was not entirely inappropriate, since, in fact, with the exception of Salazar, all Portuguese people have the surname 'da Costa'. It must be remembered that two other Portuguese surrealist painters of the time also had the same surname: António Dacosta (1914–1990) and Cândido Costa Pinto (1911–1976) but also a former president of Portugal (Gomes da Costa) and one of the assassins of King Carlos I (Afonso da Costa), for instance. The habit was continued in two or three subsequent meetings, being later forgotten.[36] Patrick Waldberg would have witnessed this episode, or heard the story later, since the idea of the Da Costa 'family' surfaces in his correspondence. This even included adding the surname to his own visiting cards and in the signature of his letters (Waldberg, M., 432).[37] The 'Da Costa' episode, and the fact that *Le Da Costa Encyclopédique* could have flowed from the *ABC*, confirms Silvano Levy's assertion that the title of the encyclopaedia was an affectionate homage to Pedro (Levy 2003, 107, endnote 134).[38]

The only publication which can be attributed, albeit somewhat controversially, to this group of London surrealists during this period is the anthology *Free Unions/Unions Libres*, whose edition was carried out individually by its secretary, Simon Watson Taylor. Published only in July 1946, it was a compilation of surrealist pieces composed during or in relation to the war, which ought to have been published in the summer of 1945. In the event, it was delayed not only due to printing problems but also to a raid by Special Branch which confiscated its content for several months.[39] Once more, despite involving the participation of many of its members, *Free Unions/Unions Libres* did not represent an example of honed collective effort, nor would it become a defining moment for this English surrealist group. Nevertheless, this is the only English publication known to contain work by Pedro, namely the aforementioned reproduction of the painting *O Repasto imundo* (*The Revolting Meal*) (1939) and an English translation of Chapter VI of *Apenas uma narrativa* (*Just a Story*) (1942) (Taylor, 6, hors-texte 24–25).

The chapter was translated by D. M. Evans, who all evidence suggests was Doreen Mary Evans, a typist and colleague of Pedro, 'employed in the office of

the Portuguese Section between 1940 and 1945'.[40] Although only this isolated
chapter came out at the time, *Apenas uma narrativa* did generate some interest,
at least in Mesens. In fact, a note at the bottom of the *Free Unions/Unions Libres*
page (Appendix 6) announces the book as forthcoming with London Gallery
Editions (a publishing outfit associated with the London Gallery, managed by
the Belgian). The full translation, carried out by the same D. M. Evans, was
revised by Pedro, who made some handwritten annotations (Appendix 7), but
it was never published. It remained in possession of Mesens, and can be found
among his papers at the Getty Research Institute in California.[41] It would be
necessary to wait almost half a century, until 1994, for another extract from
Apenas uma narrativa to be published in English: Chapter I, in a translation by
Margaret Jull Costa (Pedro 1994, 59–61).

3. The return to Portugal with suitcases full of ideas

Finding himself at odds with the strategic position adopted by the BBC regarding
ceasing commentary on matters of Portuguese internal politics, Pedro tended his
resignation effective from 31 October 1945, returning to Lisbon on 8 December
that year.[42] José Augusto França indicates that he was arrested at the border
but was released almost immediately thanks to interventions by friends and
especially by British consular staff in Portugal.[43] Pedro was aware of this danger,
as evidenced by the worry expressed by his wife and transmitted in a letter from
Adolfo Casais Monteiro regarding the likely repercussions to be expected on his
return to Portugal.[44] However he was equally certain that nothing very serious
would befall him, as is borne out by a comment by Brunius: 'il [Pedro] prétend
que désormais on n'osera plus l'arrêter, car Salazar serait paraît-il devenu prudent
pour faire bonne impression à l'étranger' ('he claims that from now on they will
no longer dare to imprison him because Salazar has become, so it seems, more
careful in order to impress the foreign community').[45]

Although this was an isolated incident, the threat of action against him by the
regime continued to loom, as Pedro himself revealed in a letter sent to Mesens
almost one year after his return: 'Ici on fait tout les possibles pour emmerder
Sardinolsar [Salazar] mais ce n'est pas facile. Je continue quand même en liberté.'
('Here one does everything to annoy Sardinlozar, but that is not easy. So far I am
keeping myself out of prison').[46] Shortly after his arrival, Pedro nonetheless had
to counter the slanderous accusation levelled at him by an anonymous article
published in the pro-Nazi newspaper *Vitória*, which suggested that he had

been 'expelled' from the BBC, and labelled him a British traitor amongst other insults.[47] Pedro immediately began legal proceedings against the newspaper's director for abuse of freedom of the press, and requested an official statement from the BBC stating that the Corporation had not instigated his departure. This act worried the British Embassy in Lisbon as to the political meaning which could be read into it and immediately pressured the BBC to suppress the truth, concerned that 'otherwise still more colour will be given to the idea, now so unfortunately current, that Great Britain was only interested in democratic principles as a propaganda stunt, and that she used Antonio Pedro until he was out of tune with her commercial aims and then threw him away'. As a result two of its directors, whom Pedro had named as witnesses, were prevented from being called to testify. Recognising that 'although his manner of leaving was, at the last moment, somewhat ungracious, his behaviour in general was strictly correct and in keeping with terms of his contract with the corporation. He did very good work throughout the period of his service', the English Corporation did not in the end issue an official declaration. Instead it sent a notarised letter to Pedro, confirming that his departure from the BBC had been entirely of his own free will, with much regret on its part.[48]

Beyond those projects already mentioned, which Pedro envisaged implementing in radio, the theatre and the press in the years following his return, two further echoes of his experiences in England can be discerned: his participation in the formal establishment of Surrealism in Portugal and his renewed commitment to painting. He devoted himself to painting with great purpose, undoubtedly impelled by the artistic context in which he had lived, above all in the surrealist group in London, and which had given him privileged access to a large variety of art exhibitions. He went on to theorise, to sketch the beginnings of grandiose paintings, albeit not completed, and to carry out further works such as the one that would come to be considered his masterpiece: *Rapto na paisagem povoada* (1946). Nevertheless Pedro would bid farewell to painting progressively, his last known canvases dating to 1950.[49] His writings on the visual arts, which had begun in the thirties, acquired more weight after his British adventure (starting with two articles praising Picasso, surely inspired by a large exhibition of his work which he had attended in London) with the publication between 1946 and 1947 of 33 instalments of his *História breve da Pintura* in *Mundo Literário* and the *Introdução a uma história de Arte: génese do fenómeno estético* (1948). The latter was also influenced by the work *Art and Society* (1937) by Herbert Read, one-time founder of the English Surrealist Group and mentor of Surrealism in

England, a man whom Pedro knew and mentioned frequently in conversation (Pedro 1946, 4).[50] But these writings were eventually likewise discontinued at the end of the 1940s.

As for Surrealism, his participation in the London group further reinforced his unparalleled status as the pioneer of the movement in Portugal. In fact his stay in England, having allowed him to break the blockade caused by war and access works by the European avant-garde, equipped him afresh with conditions to inspire others. He himself appeared with renewed vigour to the point of experimenting again, at the end of 1946, with automatic writing. He even defended for the first time automatism, a practical facet of Surrealism, "até melhor encontro, a única porta libertadora" ("until a better discovery, the only door to freedom") (Pedro 1949, 15). In 1948, he would also write one of his most surrealist poems: 'Protopoema da Serra d'Arga'. In this way, although the idea of establishing a surrealist group in Lisbon is usually attributed to Cândido Costa Pinto (1911–1976) as a result of a conversation which he had with Breton in 1947, the members involved in the process could not have done it without Pedro. Cândido himself, even before the formation of the Grupo Surrealista de Lisboa, asked Pedro to introduce his work to Mesens. Pedro duly obliged by sending a letter to the Belgian with photographs of paintings by Cândido, as well as a request on behalf of *Horizonte: jornal das artes* to obtain the right to represent the editions of the London Gallery.[51] Ironically, Pedro would again experience amongst the Lisbon surrealists similar disagreements to those which he had witnessed in the London group. The Portuguese group would suffer from the effects of excessive heterogeneity, the lack of a common action plan and, no less importantly, the different ideological positions of its members. These constraints would chafe until finally the group separated into two polar factions, just as had previously happened to the British surrealists.[52] Even the formal recognition of the group itself in Portugal would be disputed by ex-members and academics, as had been the case with the London group.

Nonetheless, it is important to remark that it was at the heart of the Grupo Surrealista de Lisboa that Pedro would again be connected to plans for an international publication: the *Revista internacional do Surrealismo*. Breton, Mesens and Nicolas Calas amongst others were to participate in the editorial team, material for the first issue was collected, however the publication never went ahead. Cited by Fátima Marinho, Mário Cesariny states that this publication would just be 'um pequeno caderno de colaborações surrealistas, portuguesas, entende-se' ('a small book of surrealist collaborations, from Portugal, that is') and that the idea sprang from his contact with Breton, Pedro having later wished to transform Cesariny's model into a publication which would represent an international version of his own *Variante* (1942–1943). Cesariny recalls further that 'com esta ideia gigante António Pedro entreteve suficientes serões, um por semana, do Grupo Surrealista de Lisboa, após o que se desinteressou da ideia, devolvendo-se a colaboração já recebida de Paris, Londres e Nova Iorque' ('with this grandiose idea António Pedro entertained a good few evenings, once a week, of the Lisbon Surrealist Group, after which he lost interest in the idea, and the contributions received from Paris, London and New York were sent back') (Marinho, 29–30).[53] Bearing in mind Pedro's trajectory in the London Surrealist Group, the frustrated *ABC* project, and knowing that he would distance himself from active Surrealism shortly after this episode, the origins of both his fervent initial interest and his later withdrawal can be understood. Out of step with the new generation, this magazine was his last attempt to create the vision of a militant Surrealism in which he believed: a space that was shared, collective and international.

In summary, Pedro's English experience would fan the flames of the main activities which he pursued in the years following his return to Portugal. Its importance for the conception and formation of a surrealist movement in Portugal is particularly noteworthy, even though Pedro was not able to avoid a repetition in Lisbon of the conflicts experienced in London. What followed from 1950s onwards is already common knowledge: Pedro's exploration became more spatial, embracing the encounter with the unifying space that the stage offered him – a space into which, in many ways, he would eventually crystallize the various dimensions of his artistic creativity.

Notes

1 Special thanks to Alastair Brotchie who very kindly drew my attention to most of these unpublished letters, in his possession, and made them available to me, some of which were already referred in his work *Encyclopaedia Acephalica: Comprising the Critical Dictionary and Related Texts* (p. 27). These are: Unpublished letter dated 10 January 1946 from Jacques-Bernard Brunius to Maurice Henry; Unpublished letter dated 10 May 1990 from Serge Senninger to Thieri Foulc; Unpublished letter dated 21 May 1992 from Edouard Jaguer to Alastair Brotchie and Unpublished letter dated 3 June [no year given] from Simon Watson Taylor to Alastair Brotchie. Four other important letters are part of *E. L. T. Mesens Papers* at the Getty Research Institute in California and *António Pedro Archive* at the Biblioteca Nacional in Lisbon.

2 'Dois anos em Londres ao serviço da BBC: António Pedro regressa a Portugal', p. 1.

3 '(Record of interview at Bush House on 4.5.45 with Pedro da Costa on the subject of his resignation withdrawal and Miss Evans' future)', *BBC Written Archives*.

4   '(H. J. Dunkerley, 10 April 1945)', *BBC Written Archives*.

5   '(Record of interview with Pedro da Costa on the subject of his proposal to change his contract from unestablished to programme contributor's, 5 April, 1945)', *BBC Written Archives*.

6   'Crónicas de 2.ª feira', *António Pedro Archives*.

7   Pedro read out the poem on 23 May 1945. The poem was later published in Portugal in 1946 with the following dedication: 'Ao António Pedro que foi na hora própria a voz de todos os portugueses que não esqueceram a sua condição de europeus e cidadãos do mundo' ('to António Pedro who was at the right time the voice of all Portuguese who had not forgotten their condition of Europeans and citizens of the world') (Monteiro, 9).

8   Interview given to *Shell News*: 'Para além do pano...', Set – Out 1949, pp. 9–10. See '(Recortes, 1945–1966)', *António Pedro Archives*.

9   'Relatório do projecto de aquisição e exploração do "Jornal do Comércio" de Lisboa', *António Pedro Archives*.

10   'Notas para o livro de Londres', *António Pedro Archives*.

11   This translation may have been carried out prior to Pedro's arrival in England. In fact, in 1943, the same publisher published two other novels by British authors translated by Pedro: *Cranford* by Elizabeth Gaskell and *The Professor* by Charlotte Brontë. Notwithstanding, an internal memo from BBC dated April 1943 detailing Pedro's professional experience mentions that 'he has therefore a good knowledge of French and little English' ('Particulars of António Pedro da Costa: 24.VIII.1943', *BBC Written Archives*). Translating English novels reveals his effort to master English, having probably in mind the possibility to travel to England and work for the BBC.

12   Chronicle of 14 August 1944. See 'Crónicas de 2.ª feira'.

13   'Quando já nem se engana o coração com música: poemas', *António Pedro Archives*. For another example of thematic and stylistic affinities between Pedro's poetry and *Apenas uma narrativa*, see also the undated poem which can be found in the archive of the surrealist E. L. T. Mesens, 'Annuaire Confidentiel', reproduced in Leão (p. 45). See especially her comments p. 42, note 3.

14   Such as Mesens, Brunius, Toni Del Renzio, Robert Melvile, Nicolas Calas, Herbert Read. Other writers and artists included Herman Hesse, Henry Matisse, Virginia Wolf, Juan Gris, Aldous Huxley, George Orwell.

15   '(From: Mr António Pedro; subject: Contribution to the magazine Horizon; To: Mr. Jeaffreson; 26.10.44)', *BBC Written Archives* and '(Lecture to the Caravela: 2nd December 1944)', *BBC Written Archives*. The article does not seem to have been published, but Pedro left a text in his archives, written in the style of a letter, in English and addressed to a man named John (most likely used by Pedro to generically represent English people). Pedro describes in it, thematically, various aspects of the history and culture of Portugal. See '(Carta a John)', *António Pedro Archives*.

16   'Dois anos em Londres ao serviço da BBC: António Pedro regressa a Portugal', p. 1.

17   Between 1944 and 1945, the participants at these gatherings varied considerably. In addition to Mesens and Brunius, Simon Watson Taylor, Serge Senninger, *Sadi Cherkeshi*, Feyyaz Fergar, the painters Robert Baxter, Emmy Bridgewater, John Banting, Eileen Agar, Edith Rimmington and later the jazz singer George Melly and the cartoonist Philip Sansom were amongst the more regular attendees. Also occasionally present were Lucien Freud, John

Craxton, Patrick Waldberg, Marie-Louise Berneri and even Robert Melville and Peter Rose-Pulham, amongst others (Jean, 335 and Walberg, P., 399).

18 '(Letter dated 23 February 1945 from Jacques-Bernard Brunius to E. L. T. Mesens)', *E. L. T. Mesens Papers*. Underlined in the original.

19 *Ibid.*

20 '(Letter dated 8 March 1945 from E. L. T. Mesens to Jacques-Bernard Brunius)', *E. L. T. Mesens Papers*. Underlined in the original.

21 *Ibid.*

22 As Serge Senninger would remember: "Da Costa était un peintre portugais, anti-Salazar du groupe surréaliste" (Unpublished letter dated 10 May 1990 from Serge Senninger to Thieri Foulc).

23 *Catalogue of Surrealist Diversity: 1915–1945*.

24 '(Cartões de divulgação da London Gallery)', *António Pedro Archives*.

25 The sale catalogue of Sotheby's features the following information: 'A Fantastic Figure and Animal in an Interior' (signed, inscribed and dated, 1944; 40.5 cm by 51 cm); 'Interior with Skeleton' (signed and dated, '44; 17 in. by 13¼ in. 43 cm by 33.5 cm); 'Hands Flying' (signed and dated 1944; 23½ in. by 19½ in. 59 cm by 49.5 cm); 'Nude Woman' (signed and dated 1945; 24½ in. by 29½ in. 62 cm by 75 cm – with the following note: 'See Illustration'); 'Head with Mushrooms' (on panel, signed, inscribed and dated 1945; 9½ in. by 12½ in. 24 cm by 32 cm); 'Hand, Dove and Wineglass' (signed, inscribed and dated '45; 15½ in. by 11½ in. 39 cm by 29 cm); 'Surrealist Composition with Nudes' (on board, signed and dated (London) '47; 17½ in. by 13½ in. 44.5 cm by 34.5 cm). All pieces were acquired by a certain 'Pereira, C.' and the final values for each painting were: £190; £180; £420; £420; £180; £400; £200 respectively. See *Catalogue of Modern British and Continental Drawings, Paintings and Sculpture: The Property of the Late E. L. T. Mesens (26 April 1972)*. 'Pássaro de mãos', exhibited in *Surrealist Diversity: 1915–1945*, might be the above mentioned 'Hands Flying'. Pedro's archives features various drawings which may be studies for these paintings. See references in *António Pedro: desenhos e manuscritos*, pp. 30–31

26 Given the war, it would have been difficult for Pedro to transport his previous paintings from Portugal to England. Besides, according to José-Augusto França, a fire in Pedro's atelier in Lisbon occurred around 1944 destroying several of his paintings (1966, 6).

27 A reproduction of the first two paintings can be found in Ávila (p. 35).

28 *Madrugada* (1940), *Natureza assassinada* (1940) and *Auto-retrato nu com uma jóia* (1943).

29 Unpublished letter dated 10 May 1990 from Serge Senninger to Thieri Foulc.

30 '(Letter dated 23 February 1945 from Jacques-Bernard Brunius to E. L. T. Mesens)'.

31 Unpublished letter dated 10 January 1946 from Jacques-Bernard Brunius to Maurice Henry.

32 Unpublished letter dated 3 June (no year given) from Simon Watson Taylor to Alastair Brotchie.

33 '(Letter from Patrick Waldberg to António Pedro)', *António Pedro Archives*. The letter is undated but its contents points to a time between October and November 1946.

34 For further details about the *Da Costa Encyclopedia*, see Kleiber.

35 'Dicionário prático ilustrado', *António Pedro Archives*

36 Unpublished letter dated 10 May 1990 from Serge Senninger to Thieri Foulc. Edouard Jaguer relates a similar version of the same story, but he gives Paris as the location, in 1947, and he identifies Breton, António Dacosta and Cândido Costa Pinto as the protagonists

(Unpublished letter dated 21 May 1992 from Edouard Jaguer to Alastair Brotchie). However, this episode takes place later than the first allusion (18 February 1946) to the Da Costa that can be found in the correspondence between Isabelle and Patrick Waldberg (Waldberg, M., 432).

37   On at least one occasion Patrick Waldberg signed a letter as 'da C'. '(Letter dated 8 January 1947 from Patrick Waldberg to E. L. T. Mesens)', *E. L. T. Mesens Papers*.

38   In an article, Raul Antelo qualifies the London surrealists as pataphysicians. However, the *Collège de 'Pataphysique* was only created in Paris at the end of 1948. A few years later, in the fifties, some ex-surrealists such as Miró, Duchamp, Ernst, Man Ray or Simon Watson Taylor would indeed became its members. Therefore, it is plausible to admit, as Alastair Brotchie suggests, a link between the volumes of *Le Memento universel Da Costa* and the founders of the *Collège de 'Pataphysique* whose identity remains a mystery. However, although a pataphysical inclination amongst the London surrealists is possible, certainly there was not a complete conscious idea of it (Antelo, 161–94 and Brotchie, *A True History*, 9–31).

39   Unpublished letter dated 3 June [no year given] from Simon Watson Taylor to Alastair Brotchie.

40   Email dated 3 June 2011 from Jeff Walden to Bruno Silva Rodrigues.

41   '(Just a Story)', *E. L. T. Mesens Papers*. The translated preface of the novel, however, is only available in Pedro's archives. 'Just a Story: preface', *António Pedro Archives*. See Appendix 8.

42   '(Pedido de demissão da BBC)', *António Pedro Archives* and Ribeiro (2013, 86–87).

43   Telephone conversation on 27 April 2011 between Bruno Silva Rodrigues and José-Augusto França.

44   '(Carta de Adolfo Casais Monteiro a António Pedro)', *António Pedro Archives*.

45   Unpublished letter dated 10 January 1946 from Jacques-Bernard Brunius to Maurice Henry.

46   '(Letter undated from António Pedro to E. L. T. Mesens)', *E. L. T. Mesens Papers*. Probably dated from the end of 1946 to March 1947.

47   'Lord Haw-Haw não foi enforcado', p. 8.

48   '(Letter dated 10 January 1946 and 17 January 1946 from Miss Withers to Communications and Broadcasting, Ministry of Information)', *BBC Written Archives* and '(Letter dated 18 January 1946 from F. B. Hills, Portuguese Section, to S. Eur. S. D.)', *BBC Written Archives*.

49   Three paintings from 1950 were recently discovered. Two were made public by a private collector and a third was found by José-Augusto França. Email dated 23 April 2011 from José Mascarenhas to Bruno Silva Rodrigues and Unpublished letter dated 2 January 2012 from José-Augusto França to Bruno Silva Rodrigues.

50   Unpublished letter dated 9 May 2011 from José-Augusto França to Bruno Silva Rodrigues. *Art and Society* had a second edition in 1945 (London) and a Portuguese translation in 1946 (Read).

51   '(Letter undated from António Pedro to E. L. T. Mesens)'.

52   Birmingham fostered a second group of English surrealists, which included Robert Melville, Conroy Maddox and Del Renzio, the latter possessing a vision of Surrealism markedly opposed to Mesens' orthodox one (Levy 2005). The age difference between Del Renzio and Mesens almost mirrors that between Mário Cesariny and Pedro, and as such the two relationships, which were broken off suddenly, present some similarities.

53   Pedro drafted the cover of this publication which has *Variante* as its title along with the

following information: '2.ª SERIE. NUMERO 1 / ANDRE BRETON. E. L. T. MESENS. NICOLAS CALAS. ANTONIO PEDRO / PARIS. NEW YORK. LONDON. LISBOA'. See '(Alfabeto)', *António Pedro Archives*.

Bibliography

Primary Sources

Pedro, A. 'Autobiografia', in *António Pedro 1909–1966* (Lisbon: Fundação Calouste Gulbenkian, 1979), pp. 54–58.

Pedro, A. 'Don Pablo Ruiz: re-inventor da pintura', *Mundo Literário*, 11 May 1946, p. 4.

Pedro, A. 'Just a Story', in *The Dedalus Book of Surrealism*, ed. by Michael Richardson, trans. by Margaret Jull Costa, 2 vols (Sawtry: Dedalus, 1994), II: *The Myth of the World*, pp. 59–61.

Pedro, A. 'Postfácio a uma actuação colectiva', in *Catálogo da exposição surrealista* (Lisbon: Cadernos surrealistas, 1949), pp. 15–16.

António Pedro Archives, Biblioteca Nacional de Portugal, Lisbon, Portugal

'(Alfabeto)', E5/298 ic.

'(Carta a John)', E5/476.

'(Carta de Adolfo Casais Monteiro a António Pedro)', E5/81.

'(Cartões de divulgação da London Gallery)', E5/583-585.

'Crónicas de 2.ª feira', E5/366-366-A.

'Dicionário prático ilustrado', E5/405-405-A.

'Notas para o livro de Londres', E5/369-369-A.

'Just a Story: preface', E5/417.

'(Letter from Patrick Waldberg to António Pedro)', E5/113.

'(Pedido de demissão da BBC)', E5/452.

'Quando já nem se engana o coração com música: poemas', E5/538.

'Relatório do projecto de aquisição e exploração do "Jornal do Comércio" de Lisboa', E5/364.

'[Recortes, 1945–1966]', E5/669.

E. L. T. Mesens Papers, Getty Research Institute, California, USA

'(Just a story)', box 14, folder 5.

'(Letter dated 8 January 1947 from Patrick Waldberg to E. L. T. Mesens)', box 6, folder 1.

'(Letter dated 8 March 1945 from E. L. T. Mesens to Jacques-Bernard Brunius)', box 9, folder 5.

'(Letter dated 23 February 1945 from Jacques-Bernard Brunius to E. L. T. Mesens)', box 9, folder 5.

'(Letter undated from António Pedro to E. L. T. Mesens)', box 9, folder 19.

BBC Written Archives, *London, UK*
'(From: Mr António Pedro; subject: Contribution to the magazine *Horizon*; To: Mr. Jeaffreson; 26.10.44)', L1/112.
'(H. J. Dunkerley, 10 April 1945)', L1/112.
'(Lecture to the Caravela: 2nd December 1944)', L1/112.
'(Letter dated 10 January 1946 and 17 January 1946 from Miss Withers to Communications and Broadcasting, Ministry of Information)', L1/112.
'(Letter dated 18 January 1946 from F. B. Hills, Portuguese Section, to S. Eur. S. D.)', L1/112.
'(Particulars of António Pedro da Costa: 24.VIII.1943)', L1/112.
'(Record of interview at Bush House on 4.5.45 with Pedro da Costa on the subject of his resignation withdrawal and Miss Evans' future)', L1/112.
'(Record of interview with Pedro da Costa on the subject of his proposal to change his contract from unestablished to programme contributor's, 5 April, 1945)', L1/112.

Secondary Sources
Agar, E., and others 'The Situation in England, the Intellectual Position With Regard to Surrealism; the Formation of an English Group; Immediate Activities', *International Surrealist Bulletin: Issued by the Surrealist Group in England*, 4 (1936), pp. 2–7.
Antelo, R. 'Antonio Pedro e a condição acefálica', *Semear*, 9 (2004), 161–94.
António Pedro: desenhos e manuscritos (Lisbon: Biblioteca Nacional, 1982).
Ávila, M. de J. and Perfecto E. C. *Surrealismo em Portugal 1934–1952* (Lisbon: Museu do Chiado, 2001).
Brotchie, A. (ed.) *Encyclopaedia Acephalica: Comprising the Critical Dictionary and Related Texts* (London: Atlas Press, 1995).
Brotchie, A. (ed.) *A True History of the College of 'Pataphysics* (London: Atlas Press, 1995).
Catalogue of Surrealist Diversity: 1915–1945 (London: Arcade Gallery, 1945).
'Dois anos em Londres ao serviço da BBC: António Pedro regressa a Portugal', *Diário de Lisboa*, 7 January 1946, p. 1.
França, J.-A. 'As Casas da areia: um texto inédito de António Pedro', *Colóquio Letras*, 115 (1990), 130–31.
França, J.-A. *A Pintura surrealista em Portugal* (Lisbon: Artis, 1966).
França, J.-A. 'O Político e o jornalista: por José-Augusto França', in *António Pedro 1909–1966* (Lisbon: Fundação Calouste Gulbenkian, 1979), pp. 43–45.
Jean, M. *The History of Surrealist Painting* (London: Weidenfeld and Nicolson, 1960).
Kleiber, P.-H. *L'Encyclopédie 'Da Costa' (1947–1949): d'acéphale au Collège de 'Pataphysique* (Lausanne: L'Age d'homme, 2014).
Leão, I. P. de 'Da dor – um percurso vital (a propósito do poema inédito de António Pedro, "Annuaire confidentiel")', *P. Portuguese Cultural Studies*, 5 (2013), 32–45, <*www2.let.uu.nl/solis/psc/p/pvolumefivepapers/p5poncedeleao.pdf*>.

Levy, S. *The Scandalous Eye: The Surrealism of Conroy Maddox* (Liverpool: Liverpool University Press, 2003).

Levy, S. The Del Renzio Affair: A Leadership Struggle in Wartime Surrealism, *Papers of Surrealism*, 3 (2005), 1–34, <http://www.surrealismcentre.ac.uk/papersofsurrealism/ journal3/acrobat_files/Levy_article.pdf>.

'Lord Haw-Haw não foi enforcado', *Vitória*, 8 January 1946, pp. 1, 8.

Marinho, M. de F. *O Surrealismo em Portugal* (Lisbon: Imprensa Nacional-Casa da Moeda, 1987).

Melly, G. *Don't Tell Sybil: An Intimate Memoir of E. L. T. Mesens* (London: Heinemann, 1997).

Monteiro, A. C. *Europa* (Lisbon: Confluência, 1946).

Ray, P. *The Surrealist Movement in England* (Ithaca: Cornell University Press, 1971).

Read, H. *Arte e sociedade*, trans. by Alberto Candeias (Lisbon: Cosmos, 1946).

Remy, M. *Surrealism in Britain* (Aldershot: Ashgate, 1999).

Ribeiro, N. 'António Pedro's 'Monday Chronicles': The Voice of Democracy on the BBC Broadcasts to Portugal During World War II', *P: Portuguese Cultural Studies*, 5 (2013), 70–90, <*www2.let.uu.nl/solis/psc/p/pvolumefivepapers/p5ribeiro.pdf*>.

Ribeiro, N. 'Political Interference on the Airwaves: The BBC Broadcasts to Portugal during the Second World War', *Westminster Papers in Communication and Culture*, 7 (2), 2010, 122–39.

Catalogue of Modern British and Continental Drawings, Paintings and Sculpture: The Property of the Late E. L. T. Mesens [26 April 1972] (London: Sotheby and Co, 1972).

Taylor, S. W. (ed.) *Free Unions/Unions Libres* (London: Express Printers, 1946).

Waldberg, M. (ed.) *Un amour acéphale: correspondance 1940–1949* (Paris: Éditions de la différence, 1992).

Waldberg, Patrick, *Les Demeures d'Hypnos* (Paris: Éditions de la différence, 1976).

Unpublished sources

Email dated 23 April 2011 from José Mascarenhas to Bruno Silva Rodrigues.

Email dated 3 June 2011 from Jeff Walden to Bruno Silva Rodrigues.

Telephone Conversation on 27 April 2011 Between Bruno Silva Rodrigues and José-Augusto França.

Unpublished letter dated 10 January 1946 from Jacques-Bernard Brunius to Maurice Henry.

Unpublished letter dated 10 May 1990 from Serge Senninger to Thieri Foulc.

Unpublished letter dated 21 May 1992 from Edouard Jaguer to Alastair Brotchie.

Unpublished letter dated 9 May 2011 from José-Augusto França to Bruno Silva Rodrigues.

Unpublished letter dated 2 January 2012 from José-Augusto França to Bruno Silva Rodrigues.

Unpublished letter dated 3 June [no year given] from Simon Watson Taylor to Alastair Brotchie.

JUST A STORY

APENAS UMA NARRATIVA

'Meu Dislate a conventos longos orça'

Mário de Sá-Carneiro

PREFÁCIO

Hesitei muito antes de dar um título ao que vai seguir-se. Há pessoas que julgam os títulos de somenos importância, coisa que depois terá sua razão de ser na continuação da leitura. Há outras pessoas que depois de terem feito um livro pegam no nome duma das personagens e escrevem-no com letra mais grossa na capa, como se bastasse. As primeiras funcionam como os provérbios, as segundas como os padrinhos. Ambas estão erradas, como não podia deixar de ser. Os provérbios podem ser aplicados assim como nos lembram ou ao contrário e estão sempre bem. É essa a razão da sabedoria popular ou daquilo que assim se chama e é ingenuidade e, por consequência, o contrário da sabedoria. Os nomes que os padrinhos dão a uma criança, quando chega o momento de ser necessário designá-la, são sempre tão mal escolhidos que a gente de casa passa logo a chamar-lhe um diminutivo qualquer e, quando cresce, a gente de fora passa sempre a chamá-la pelo apelido, que é o nome do pai com quem entende que deve parecer-se por uma razão de hereditariedade. Os padrinhos só acertam por acaso e estes acasos felizes são exceções que não fazem senão confirmar a regra que lhes é contrária.

Não foi portanto fácil a escolha deste título ou, mais verdadeiramente, não teria sido fácil se ele fosse verdadeiramente um título. O que vai ler-se é apenas uma narrativa *daquilo que não aconteceu, como deve ser em todos os romances. Chama- -se portanto aquilo que é, embora não seja costume.*

Outro facto que talvez mereça os reparos iniciais que justificam a existência dos prefácios é a designação de romance*. No Brasil, aqui há tempos, houve uma grande discussão entre escritores acerca do que devia chamar-se romance, do que devia chamar-se novela e do que devia chamar-se conto. Todos tinham tanta razão com seus argumentos que só um a teve a ponto de não valer a pena falar-se mais no assunto. Uns optavam pela questão do tamanho, outros pela questão do conteúdo, outros pela maneira de contar as coisas. Creio ser de Mário de Andrade a justa teoria:*

– Romance é aquilo que o seu autor resolveu designar assim.

A história que vai ler-se é simples como as plantas e nasceu como elas naturalmente, embora, como elas, tenha por vezes formas inesperadas. Não tem intenção de provar

'My Folly to lengthy cloisters amounts'

Mário de Sá-Carneiro

PREFACE

I thought long and hard before giving a title to the story that follows. Some people consider titles to be of little importance, for they only gain their value as the reading of the story progresses. Some write a book, then take the name of one of its characters and write it in bolder letters on the cover, as if that were good enough. The first class of titles functions as proverbs, the second as godparents. Both are wrong, of course. Proverbs can be used as we wish, or to state the opposite, and they still make sense. That is what lies behind popular wisdom or what passes for it, and it is naive and, therefore, the opposite of wise. The names godparents give a child, when the time comes to do so, are always so badly chosen that the family soon begins to call the child some nickname or other and, when the child grows, other people always use a surname, the father's name, since the child should be similar to the father owing to heredity. The godparents are only ever right by chance, these fortunate accidents being the exceptions which only confirm the rule.

It was not easy, therefore, to chose a title for this book; or, more accurately, it would not have been easy were it really a title. What you will read is just a story of what didn't happen, as should be the case with every novel. It is therefore called what it is, however unusual this may be.

Another topic that merits the initial remarks that justify the existence of prefaces is the novel's genre. In Brazil, a while back, there was a great discussion amongst writers concerning what should be called a novel, what should be called a novella, and what should be called a short story. Each writer was so convincing in his arguments that it soon became pointless to discuss the matter further. Some distinguished between them according to length, others by content, or storytelling technique. I believe it was Mário de Andrade who quite rightly theorised:

A novel is something its author decided to call a novel.

The story that follows is as simple as plants and was born, like plants, naturally, even though, like plants, it sometimes takes on surprising shapes. It does not aim to prove

coisa nenhuma mas, se a tivesse, seria a de que há uma lógica do absurdo tão verdadeira, pelo menos, como a lógica racional, embora muito mais espontaneamente aceitável do que ela e, se não fosse perigoso tocar em tais questões, muito mais parecida com aquela que usam os artistas que o povo entende: oleiros de romaria que fazem gatos dourados com manchas vermelhas e cara de gente, contistas de serão provinciano que inventam histórias da carochinha, e aquele poeta extraordinário e desconhecido que inventou o rico pico serenico quem te deu tamanho bico ou de ouro ou de prata mete aqui nesta buraca.

Resumindo pois, o que vai seguir-se, porque é narrado de forma sem pretensões, é Apenas uma narrativa *e, porque assim me pareceu bem, subintitula-se* Romance.

A quem não cheguem estas explicações, absolutamente desnecessárias, recomenda--se que não leia este livro. Aos outros também, por modéstia obrigatória, sem nenhuma convicção.

O autor

DEDICATÓRIA

AO SENHOR AQUILINO RIBEIRO

MESTRE:

Toda a gente vai ficar espantada com a dedicatória deste livro e com este invocativo que tomo em gosto tornar público, não com sanha de discípulo que não sou, mas com respeito de homem de ofício que sabe quem no merece. Toda a gente vai ficar espantada e pouco isso me importaria se entre essa "toda a gente" não estivesse, como está por certo, o meu Amigo. Eis a razão porque não honro apenas com o seu nome esta folha e me parece necessário explicar--lhe porque o faço.

Há ainda quem tenha a mania de distinguir arte moderna e arte antiga e quem nesta distinção se compraza, ou viva desta distinção. Aqui, público e raso, me confesso do pecado de a ter já feito para tornar mais clara certa confusão entre bom e mau. O que há com arte, com artistas e com tudo, cabe apenas nestas duas espécies. O meu Amigo é dos bons e eu faço por merecer--lhe a companhia. O resto são diferenças que dizem respeito à sua educação e à minha, ao seu gosto e ao meu, à sua Beira de desvirgadas, padres, lobos e almocreves e ao meu Minho de cantorias e emigrantes, milho verde, leiras

anything but, if it did, it would prove that there exists a logic of the absurd that is as true as rational logic, if not more so, although the latter is much more readily accepted and, were it not for the danger of touching on such matters, much closer to the logic of the artists whom ordinary people understand: potters of pilgrimages who make golden cats with red stains and human faces, town storytellers who invent fairy tales, and that extraordinary, unknown poet who invented the woody woodpecker tongue twister.[1]

In short, what follows is Just a Story *because it is told with no pretension and, because I saw fit, its subtitle is* A Novel.

If you are not satisfied with these explanations, which are completely unnecessary, I recommend you don't read the book. I actually recommend this to everyone, with the obligatory modesty, and with no conviction.

The author

DEDICATION

TO MR AQUILINO RIBEIRO

MASTER:
Everyone will be surprised by this book's dedication and my pleasure in making it public, not in the spirit of a disciple, which I'm not, but with the respect of a working man who knows who is worthy of such a gesture. Everyone will be surprised and I wouldn't care were it not for the fact that you, my Friend, are one of that everyone. That's why I not only honour your name on this page, but find it necessary to explain why I do so.

There are still some people who insist on distinguishing between modern and ancient art, and who enjoy this distinction, or live by it. Here, publicly and humbly, I confess to the sin of having made the distinction myself, in order to clear up certain confusions between what is good and what is bad. Art, artists and everything else fall into these two categories. You, my Friend, are one of the good ones, and I endeavour to be worthy of your company. Everything else is the difference between your education and my own, your taste and mine, your Beira of deflowered virgins, priests, wolves and shepherds, and my Minho of

---

[1] In the original, this sentence is followed by a tongue-twister about a woodpecker: 'pico serenico quem te deu tamanho bico ou de ouro ou de prata mete aqui nesta buraca.'

pequenas, pedinchas, sovinas e fantasmas líricos; o resto, e sobretudo, são coisas que dizem respeito àquelas pulgas que cada um tem seu modo de matar; o resto, ainda, perdoe-me dizer-lho, tem com a sua idade e com a minha idade. E se, com tão oposta educação estética, tão diferente gosto, cenário de infância tão díspar, tão discrepante forma de matar pulgas, idade para ser seu filho, quiser saber porque o admiro, deixe-me lembrar-lhe que escreveu o romance da raposa raposeca, senhora de muita treta, e do galo galaroz, perninhas de retroz, que contou como era a terceira classe da arca de Noé e, também, às vezes, se deixa empapar em sonho, como ninguém, em certas páginas da Aventura Maravilhosa e de outros livros – um sonho por vezes revesso nas palavras saborosas que só tolos veem por fora, como chuvinha bonita em que não sabem molhar-se.

Não há arte moderna nem antiga. Os artistas é que são modernos e antigos com relação ao momento, e os antigos para o seu momento são sempre maus e sempre errados. O seu momento, Aquilino Ribeiro, ninguém o honrou como V. Foi a volta à terra depois da especulação, a volta ao gosto infantil depois da pedagogia parva, a volta ao sonho e à epopeia depois da crítica e da caricatura. A Academia com que o insultaram (e em que companhias, Deus do céu!) mais a mereciam certos *modernos* que conhecemos – soldados uniformizados, como os outros, satisfeitos de abotoarem o mesmo dólman com botõezinhos de outra cor.

Lisboa, novembro de 1941

popular songs and migrants, unripe corn, small furrows, beggars, misers and lyric ghosts; everything else relates to the fleas we all have our different ways of killing; everything else, at the end of the day, and forgive me for saying so, has to do with our difference in age. And if I, having such a different aesthetic education, such different tastes and childhood memories, such different ways of killing fleas, am young enough to be your son, please know that I admire you, and let me remind you that you wrote the novel of the sneaky fox and the cocky cock, you described what it was like in the third class of Noah's ark and also, sometimes, allowed yourself to dream, like no one else, in certain pages of the *Wonderful Adventure* and other books[2] – a dream which is often enclosed in the delicious words fools only see from the outside, like the lovely small rain they don't know how to enjoy.

There is no such thing as modern or ancient art. Artists are only modern or ancient in relation to their time, and the ancients in relation to their time are always bad and always wrong. Your moment, Aquilino Ribeiro, was celebrated by you more than anyone. It marked the return to earth after speculation, the return to childish pleasures after foolish pedagogy, the return to dreams and epics after criticism and caricature. The Academy they insulted you with (placing you in what company, dear God!) would be better served by certain *moderns* we know – uniformed soldiers, like the others, content to button up the same coat with differently coloured buttons.[3]

Lisbon, November 1941

---

[2] References to Aquilino Ribeiro's novels *O Romance da Raposa* (*The Fox's Novel*) (1924), *Arca de Noé I, II* and *III* [*Noah's Ark*], and *Aventura Maravilhosa* (*The Wonderful Adventure*) (all 1936).

[3] Aquilino Ribeiro was elected a member of the *Academia das Ciências de Lisboa* (Lisbon Academy of Sciences) in 1935.

CAPÍTULO I

CHAPTER ONE

O plantador chamava-se Adão, como é fácil de calcular.

The farmer was called Adam, as you may have gathered.

O rio Minho tem um afluente que se chama Coura e nasce entre pedras como um fio de água. Andam-lhe à roda pinheiros distraídos debaixo do céu, que é sempre azul e luminoso, e matam nele a sede os lobos e as rolas. A água corre sem ter tempo de colher estas imagens, feita espuma, de penhasco em penhasco. Vai engrossando, sem se saber bem porquê, no declive da montanha e, à medida que desce e aumenta, vai-se tornando mais séria. Começa por brinquedo que serve de brinquedo a algumas rãs, acaba em paisagem, já com recantos românticos onde se espelham as árvores e onde navegam trutas, mujos e enguias. Ao meio deste crescendo há um engenho de açudes, para colher energia elétrica, que fica ridículo com seu ar industrial entre aquelas sombras. Também às vezes há regueiras naturais que estagnam ali paradas, por engano, num refego do terreno, e outras de propósito para servir às terras de semeadura. Andam pássaros, moscas e tira-olhos, numa azáfama, sobre tudo isto. Creio que foi no princípio do mundo que assim se estabeleceram as coisas. Foi há muito tempo mas, à exceção da indústria, tudo conserva um ar inicial, como era necessário.

Acompanhando o leito do rio há pequenos plainos aráveis que terminam em degrau, até ao mais baixo onde se estende a planície. O plantador andava ali, pelo campo, enterrado até acima dos joelhos, na terra que é ubérrima e preta. Era bonito vê-lo andar nu, o rosado do corpo a contrastar com a cor dos torrões remexidos, lançando ao longo das leivas aqueles bocados de mulher que levava num braçado. Havia braços de rainhas de mãos pendentes, brancas e com anéis, rosários de olhos como bolindros variegados com ternuras incalculáveis e molhadas e também com ódios e estupidez, mitras e cogumelos, como anémonas que, se tinham nascido e morrido era por acaso, ao sabor do vaivém do sangue, na pele sei lá de quem. Também havia pernas e bocas, ossinhos brancos e dentes e também havia cabelos no que ele levava de braçado. Via-se que era um hábito seu aquela espécie de sementeira e, se na verdade o não era, assim parecia, enquadrado no ambiente bucólico do entardecer que, naquela parte do Minho, tem um encanto de paraíso.

Quando acabou o dia e recolheram os pássaros, se calaram as cantigas e passaram para Espanha os patos, as aves frias que voam alto e toda a outra arribação, o plantador deitou-se sobre a terra e acendeu a lua como uma lamparina para acompanhar-lhe o sono merecido. Quase não havia estrelas e tudo seria silêncio se não fosse o latir dos cães que se pressentia na aldeia ao lado.

Com a noite, o acento romântico deste conjunto ganhou valores de magia, mas chegou um tempo em que todo aquele romantismo se tornou inaceitável.

The Minho River has a tributary called the Coura, which bubbles up from the stones as a trickle of water. Distracted pine trees surround it under the blue, luminous sky, and wolves and doves quench their thirst in it. The water flows from rocky ledge to rocky ledge, turning into foam, having no time to gather these images. It thickens, for no apparent reason, in the lower slopes of the mountain, and as it descends and swells, it becomes more serious. It begins as a toy for toads to play with, it ends in scenery, with romantic corners where it reflects the trees, and where trout, mullet and eels swim. In the midst of this crescendo is a weir to produce electricity, looking ridiculously industrial amongst the shadows. Sometimes, too, there are natural ditches, lying stagnant, forgotten in a hollow of ground, and others built to irrigate the fields. Birds, flies and dragonflies fly busily above all this. I believe things were made just so when the earth was created. That was a very long time ago but, apart from industrialisation, everything looks as it did in the beginning, as it should.

Following the riverbed are small arable terraces which end in steps, the lowest where the plain begins. The farmer walked there, in the fields, buried to above his knees in the rich, dark earth. It was pleasant to see him naked, his rosy body contrasting with the colour of the new-turned clods, flinging the pieces of woman he carried in his arms along the furrows. There were queens' arms with drooping hands, white and jewelled, rosaries of eyes like multicoloured marbles, moist and full of incalculable tendernesses, but also hatreds and stupidities, mitres and mushrooms, like anemones which were born and died by chance, at the mercy of the flowing blood under I don't know whose skin. There were also legs and mouths, small white bones and teeth and hair. You could tell that this type of sowing was a habit of his, or if indeed it wasn't it appeared to be, in the bucolic atmosphere of the late afternoon which, in that part of Minho, is as charming as paradise.

When the day ended and the birds went to roost, when the singing stopped and the ducks, the cold birds that fly high above and all the other birds flew over to Spain, the farmer lay down on the ground and switched on the moon like a lantern to accompany his well earnt sleep. There were hardly any stars out and all would have been silent save for the faint barking of dogs from the neighbouring village.

As night fell, the romantic feel of all this gained magical qualities, but there came a time when so much romanticism became unacceptable. The things sown

As coisas semeadas desfizeram-se em húmus e o homem acordou pegado à terra, como as árvores de ao pé da água, alimentado duma seiva a que não estava habituado. Mercê de tal alimento cresceu a todo o tamanho do céu, até ficar mais alto do que a noite.

Tudo se passou tão de repente que se sentiu tonto da altura e teve vertigens como não sabia. A cabeça andava-lhe à roda. Do movimento e da agonia desarticulou-se-lhe o pescoço. Depois rebentaram-lhe as veias todas pela pressão da altitude. Foi imponente como uma catarata e mais espetaculoso por causa da cor.

O minhoto é amador de romarias e de festas de fogo-de-artifício. Toda a gente veio ver aquela subida do homem e aquele desabar, lá de cima, de sangue vermelho em catadupas, a refletir-se no rio com os revérberos da lua. Mas aquilo durou pouco. Seco da seiva ficou-lhe a carne de palha e sem mais préstimo nenhum. Ao fim de poucas semanas já nem reparavam nele, como se não passasse dum espantalho maior. Quando acabaram as colheitas deitaram--lhe fogo como ao restolho. Na sua cinza mijaram os gatos e espojaram-se as galinhas. Só a sombra que tinha feito ficou no chão como uma nódoa.

Era uma mancha verde-escura, longa como um descampado.

Houve diversas discussões se havia ou não que retirá-la dali por causa do turismo e do bom nome da localidade. Uns eram partidários do pitoresco e outros queriam as coisas como deviam ser. Durante a contenda apareceu até quem não quisesse acreditar que a sombra não era uma coisa natural. Acabaram por enrolá-la, como a um tapete, e levá-la para observação dos membros da Academia.

Cheirava tanto a tristeza que os académicos se acharam comovidos. Escreveu então, cada um, seu soneto comemorativo. Desse conjunto de produções literárias da melhor água se fez e se editou um livro que aí corre e não tem, evidentemente, nada de comum com esta história verdadeira.

O plantador chamava-se Adão, como é fácil de calcular. Não é, no entanto, verdade que fosse o primeiro homem. Antes e depois dele já havia este sabor a vazio que enche o mundo duma inquietação sem remédio.

dissolved into rich soil and the man awoke clinging to the earth, like trees near water, an unfamiliar sap flowing through his veins. Thanks to this nourishment, he grew as big as the sky, until he was taller than the night.

Everything happened so quickly that he felt giddy from the height and suffered terrible vertigo. His head was spinning. His neck snapped from the movement and the agony. Then his veins burst from the altitude. It was as impressive as a waterfall and more spectacular, because of the colour.

The people of Minho love their religious festivals and firework displays. Everyone gathered to see the man's ascent and fall, from high above, in cataracts of red blood, reflected on the moonlit river below. But it didn't last long. Drained of sap, his flesh became nothing but useless straw. A few weeks later no one noticed him any longer, as if he were just a giant scarecrow. When the harvest was over they set fire to him, as to stubble. Cats pissed on his ashes, and chickens rolled about in them. Only the shadow he had cast remained on the ground, like a stain.

It was a dark green stain, as long as a wasteland.

There were lengthy discussions as to whether or not to remove it for the sake of the tourist trade and the area's reputation. Some favoured the picturesque, others wanted things to be as they should be. During these debates there were even those who refused to believe that the shadow was supernatural. They finally rolled it up like a rug, and took it to the members of the Academy for observation.

It smelt so much of sadness that the academicians were moved. Each one then penned his commemorative sonnet. Those first-rate literary products were put in a book which still survives and does not have, of course, anything to do with this true story.

The farmer was called Adam, as you may have gathered. He was not, however, the first man. Before and after him there was already this empty feeling that fills the world with an incurable restlessness.

CAPÍTULO II

CHAPTER TWO

Da água do lago nasceu um caule desmedido.

A great tree trunk grew from the waters of the lake

Foi no lugar da sombra do plantador que construíram uma vila a que se deu, por ternura, o nome de Caminha. É uma vila triste como nenhuma outra porque a sua tristeza é sem razão. Quando lhe bate o sol, as casas, que são caiadas, brilham entre os cunhais de granito acinzentado como lágrimas entre as pestanas, e não se sabe nunca se é de gosto ou de desgosto a sua evidente comoção. Tudo é pequeno e aconchegado, tudo é suave e parece bonito na imagem que se espelha nos dois rios que a envolvem – coxas refletoras de que ela é o sexo virgem: as ruas são irregulares e limpas e, de dentro das casas, saem pragas de pescador, risos e cantigas, ruído de escarros e o mau falar dos contrabandistas, louvores ao Senhor e conversa de comadres; há duas pontes galantes e um passeio com choupos à beira d'água, uma igreja românica com uma porta da morte e uma gárgula que faz manguitos aos espanhóis, ameias velhas, uma torre séria com um relógio e um chafariz bordado em pedra enegrecida com elegâncias de bailarino; há estas coisas e mais, e ainda uma cortina de montes com pinheiros verdes, como cabelos, e rochas e terra castanha, tudo coberto do doirado da luz que se entremeia em tudo... e, no entanto, a vila é triste como nenhuma outra, talvez porque foi nela que eu nasci.

Nasci antes da guerra que vem no Apocalipse, em casa que estava isolada num alto de colina. A casa era um solar antigo, de salas desconformes, onde só se podia estar abandonado. Tinha os tetos de madeira pintados com santos e com folhas. Cheirava sempre a todos os mortos que estiveram cerimoniosamente lá dentro, em câmara ardente, desde a fundação da monarquia, e tinha uma cadeira de braços forrada de veludo verde. Por fora havia o quintal.

Quando começou aquela guerra medonha, no quintal da nossa casa só havia flores e pássaros. As flores e os pássaros eram em tal quantidade que até parecia não haver terra nem ar. Os pássaros enchiam o céu todo, uns contra os outros, tão encostados que só podiam deslocar-se em conjunto. Era lindo vê-los como um enorme corpo multiforme e multicor encher de reflexos as flores que estavam em baixo e eram tantas e tão altas que, partindo do chão e cobrindo-o por completo, lhes chegavam com as corolas. Seria difícil distinguir uma coisa da outra se não fosse pelo movimento poder estabelecer-se a diferença – as flores estavam quietas, os pássaros, esses, andavam naquele balanço que lhes sugeria o hábito de voar.

No quintal, é claro, não caberia mais nada se não fosse a clareira do lago e um buraco que a lua abrira para lá chegar através do maciço dos pássaros. O buraco da lua parecia uma ferida branca mas era bonito como uma seda velha. Tudo era bonito no quintal da nossa casa quando começou aquela guerra medonha!

A town was built on the site of the farmer's shadow. It was named Caminha, for sentimental reasons. It is the saddest town in the world, because its sadness has no reason to be. When the sun shines down on it, the whitewashed houses sparkle amongst the greyish granite crags, like tears between eyelashes, and it's impossible to tell whether their evident emotion is one of love or heartbreak. Everything is small and snug, everything looks peaceful and pretty in the scene mirrored in the two rivers that embrace the town, like reflective thighs around its virgin sexual parts: the streets are irregular and clean and fishermen's curses, laughter and songs, the sound of spitting and smugglers' swearing, praises to God and the gossip of townswomen come from the houses; there are two pretty bridges and a footpath, edged by poplars, on the riverbank, a Romanesque church with a death gate and a gargoyle making obscene gestures at the Spaniards, old battlements, a sombre tower with a clock and a fountain surrounded by black stone with statues of dancers; there are these things and more, including a curtain of hills with green pine trees for hair, and rocks and brown earth, all bathed in the golden light that filters through everything... and yet it's the saddest town in the world, perhaps because it's the town I was born in.

I was born before the war of the Apocalypse, in an isolated house on a hilltop. It was an old manor house, with huge rooms where one could only feel abandoned. Its wooden ceilings were decorated with paintings of saints and leaves. It always smelt of the dead people who had once ceremoniously been inside, lying in state, since the foundation of the monarchy, and there was an armchair upholstered with green velvet. Outside there was a yard.

When that fearsome war began, our house's yard was full of flowers and birds. There were so many flowers and birds that there seemed to be no earth or air. The birds took up the whole sky, one pressed against the other, so close they could only move in unison. It was lovely to watch that huge multiform, multicoloured body cast reflections on the flowers below, which were so numerous and tall, covering the whole ground, that they reached up with their petals to touch the birds. It would have been difficult to distinguish birds from flowers were it not for their movement – the flowers were still, while the birds' swinging back and forth suggested their habit of flying.

Nothing else would have fit in the yard, of course, were it not for the lake clearing, and a hole the moon pierced through the mass of birds in order to reach it. The hole the moon made looked like a white wound but was as pretty as a piece of old silk. Everything in our house's yard house was beautiful when that fearsome war began!

No lago, a água era como de costume: parecia sensível e, a cada arrepio, enchia-se de rodas como para brincar. Lembro-me das correrias que fazia com essas rodas, cada vez maiores, quando as tirava do lago e as impelia com um arame niquelado na alameda do pinheiral cheia de árvores velhinhas – umas árvores que bebiam sol como se fosse aguardente e me contavam por vezes, ao entardecer, as histórias mais lindas que eu já ouvi contar. Foi neste pinhal do Camarido que todas elas desapareceram, sumidas no ar que é mais leve que a respiração, quando eu lhes confundia o brilho com o das moscas que são azuis e têm luzes de humidade.

Depois veio a catástrofe. Havia dois exércitos de esfomeados, um de cada lado do quintal. Eram ambos de homens barbudos, musculosíssimos e horríveis, e ambos sabiam tudo o que é preciso saber para se fazer bem a guerra. Quando um exército embateu contra o outro exército esmagaram o que havia no meu quintal.

Lutaram por muito tempo. Quase não faziam barulho. Só se ouvia, por todos os lados, aquele ruído de esforço que faz o ar ao escapar-se pela garganta, quando se puxa, com violência, uma machadada.

Foi um horror! O chão ficou coberto duma pasta esbranquiçada como a cor do caminho da lua, mas muito menos sentimental nos reflexos e muito menos transparente. Com a morte dos pássaros, o ar voltou a ocupar o que fora o quintal da nossa casa, e com ele a desolação.

Da água do lago nasceu um caule desmedido. Ficou ali a refletir-se como uma coisa agoirenta. Quando chegou a primavera nasceram-lhes olhos como folhas. Os olhos choraram para o lago como o chafariz da vila. O lago transbordou e inundou o quintal.

Durante o tempo em que isto se passava, com o medo e com o espanto, os membros tinham-se-me colado ao corpo transformando-me numa coisa imóvel e sem remédio. Estive assim até que a água chegou acima do nível dos soalhos e pôs a boiar a poltrona forrada de veludo verde onde eu ficara transido, despegando-me por fim os braços e as pernas da incómoda e inútil atitude involuntária.

Só então consegui fazer com um jornal aquele barco de papel que me haviam ensinado e em que pude fugir ao sabor da aragem que era fresca e vinha puxada do norte.

Eu era pequeno e acreditava em milagres, mas, com a humidade, as letras do jornal marcaram-me a pele, ao acaso, duma maneira insuportável. Foi por onde calhou e fiquei ridículo como é fácil imaginar. Dessas marcas, umas levou-mas

The lake's waters were the usual ones: they seemed sensitive and, at every shudder of wind, became full of ripples, as if wanting to play. I remember racing against those ripples, which grew bigger and bigger as I removed them from the lake and threw them, with a nickel wire, against the avenue of ancient pine trees – trees that drank sunlight as if it were liquor and who sometimes told me the most moving stories I have ever heard, at dusk. When I mistook their sparkle for that of blue flies with their humid lights, they all disappeared in this Camarido wood, into the air that is lighter than breath.

Then came the catastrophe. There were two starving armies, one on either side of the yard. Both consisted of bearded men, muscular and horrible, and both knew everything there is to know about war. When the armies clashed, they crushed everything in my yard.

They fought a long time, almost in silence. On those lands one could only hear the sound a breath makes escaping a throat, as a man wields an axe with great force.

It was horrific! A whitish paste the colour of the moon's path, but far less sentimental in its reflections and much less transparent, covered the earth. When the birds died, the air once again occupied what had been the yard of our house, and with it desolation.

A great tree trunk grew from the waters of the lake. It stayed there, reflecting itself like something ominous. In the spring it grew eyes like leaves. The eyes cried into the lake, like the town fountain. The lake overflowed and flooded the yard.

While this was happening, my limbs stuck to my body owing to the fear and shock, turning me into a motionless, useless thing. I remained like that, petrified, until the water rose above the floorboards and made the green velvet armchair, in which I sat drenched, float. This finally released my arms and legs from their uncomfortable, helpless involuntary position.

It was only then that I was able to fashion, out of newspaper, the paper boat they had taught me to make, and I escaped with the cool northern breeze.

I was young and believed in miracles but, owing to the humidity, the newspaper's letters tattooed my skin randomly, unbearably. They stuck where they happened to be and I looked ridiculous, as one can imagine. Some of those

o tempo, outras gastaram-se felizmente com este hábito que ganhei de me roçar pelos rochedos e pelas árvores à busca duma calma que não vem.

De toda esta aventura só me resta numa coxa um anúncio que parece sem importância. Tem um risco preto à volta e diz assim:

> LULU
>
> Sem notícias. Vem às 5. Muitos b.
> do teu até à morte.
>
> ....

Sumiu-se a letra da assinatura. O resto, julguei eu, também havia de acabar por desvanecer... mas, afinal, para a minha vida teve as mais graves consequências.

marks were erased over time, others were fortunately rubbed off by my habit of brushing against rocks and trees, searching for an unattainable peace.

All I am left with, from this whole adventure, is a seemingly insignificant advert on one of my thighs. It is surrounded by a black box, and it reads:

LULU

No news. Come at 5. Many
kisses from yours until death.

....

The letters of the signature have disappeared. The rest, I thought, would fade away too… however, the advert had the gravest consequences for my life.

CAPÍTULO III

CHAPTER THREE

*…a Lulu andava na rua com os olhos de toda a gente pegados
às diversas partes do seu corpo fresquíssimo…*

*…everyone's eyes were glued to the different parts of Lulu's alluring body
as she walked down the street…*

A Lulu tinha um costume tão desagradável como uma impigem e muito mais extraordinário. Quando saía à rua havia pessoas que lhe diziam que ela era muito fresca e de tal maneira se convenceu disso e cultivou a sua frescura que as pessoas, quando passava, não tinham outro remédio senão dizer-lhe que a achavam muito fresquíssima, de modo a fazê-la ficar absolutamente satisfeita. Tudo isto parecia poder confinar-se a um simples jogo de sociedade. O pior era que, quando ela ficava absolutamente satisfeita na rua, em casa a satisfação não era tanta que se não pusesse em frente do espelho a imaginar a maneira de conseguir, para o dia seguinte, muito mais expressão na forma como lhe dirigiam as amabilidades. Chegou um momento em que se tornou tão difícil a forma como se lhe haviam de dirigir as amabilidades que a única amabilidade possível era só uma expressão, mesmo sem dizer nada para não sair asneira.

Era assim de inverno mas era sobretudo assim na época de verão, quando mais nos apetece mandar rapar a erva e os musgos que o tempo cria na pele e onde nos escorregam os gestos como que cansados.

Desta maneira a Lulu andava na rua com os olhos de toda a gente pegados às diversas partes do seu corpo fresquíssimo, tão radiante por isso lhe acontecer, que seria uma pena alguém dizer-lhe qualquer coisa de razoável. Ninguém, de resto, pensava nisso, e até as pessoas de maior moralidade perdoavam a provocação pela beleza do espetáculo que oferecia aquela rapariga tão agradável, toda coberta de olhos. Ela, quando chegava a casa, despegava-os com imenso cuidado e metia-os numa caixinha de cartão, espetados em alfinetes, como se estivesse fazendo uma coleção de borboletas.

Correu tudo muito bem até ao dia em que a Lulu já não sabia o que havia de fazer àquela porção de olhos que na rua se pegavam ao seu corpo fresquíssimo, e o número de caixas era tal que resolveu ficar em casa para escolher, com paciência, qual seria afinal, daqueles todos, o predileto. Não foi um trabalho fácil. Ia destapando as caixinhas de cartão e aconchegando os que estavam mal arrumados enquanto comparava, com certo comprazimento, os seus entusiasmos e simpatias, até que viu luzir mais apetecivelmente certo olho preto que devia ter pertencido a sobrancelhas daquelas aveludadas e tudo.

Ficou um tanto comovida e até se tomou dum tal ou qual constrangimento quando deu conta dessa sensação, mas breve se refez. Arrancou com muito cuidado o alfinete finíssimo que lhe tinha espetado para o guardar, e pô-lo em frente de si, disposta a dar-lhe a vantagem de ser ele, um dia inteiro, a mirá-la sozinho, cada vez mais fresca.

Lulu had a habit as unpleasant as a rash, and far less common. When she went out, some people would tell her she looked very alluring, and she became so convinced of the fact, and so cultivated her allure, that people, when she passed, had no choice but to tell her that they found her very alluring, which made her completely satisfied.

All this may appear to be a simple game of society. The problem is that, after she was completely satisfied on the street, when she got home she was not satisfied enough to prevent her from standing before a mirror, pondering how she might inspire even more enthusiastic compliments the following day. There came a point when it became so difficult to pay her compliments that the only possible one was a single, wordless gesture, so as to avoid saying the wrong thing.

This happened in winter but especially in summer, when we most feel like razing the undergrowth and moss which time grows on our skin, and when we cannot control our actions, through weariness.

In this way, everyone's eyes were glued to the different parts of Lulu's alluring body as she walked down the street. She was so happy about this that it would be a shame for anyone to tell her anything sensible. No one, indeed, gave it a second thought, and the more morally-minded people forgave the provocative beauty of the spectacle that delectable girl, all covered in gazes, created. As for her, when she got home she unglued the gazes with the utmost care and pinned them in a cardboard box, as if she were collecting butterflies.

Everything went smoothly until the day Lulu no longer knew what to do with all the eyes that stuck to her alluring body on the street, and there were so many boxes that she decided to stay home to patiently choose her favourite. It was no easy feat. She opened the little cardboard boxes and re-arranged the untidy ones while she compared, with a certain complaisance, their ardours and charms, until she spied a certain dark eye, which must have belonged to velvety eyebrows, shining more attractively than the others.

She was so moved that she became uncomfortable at her own emotion, but she soon composed herself. She carefully removed the eye from its thin pin, placing it in front of her to allow it the honour of being the only one to gaze at her ever more alluring body for an entire day.

Para lhe agradar completamente e lhe dar toda a medida da sua graça pôs-se a cantar estas palavras que lhe vieram à boca com uma música muito harmoniosa:

> Rico mico saltarico,
> Minha boca fez um bico,
> Desse bico fiz a bola
> Que te jogo e que rebola
> E que dança o bailarico
> Ao som da minha viola,
> Ao som do meu cavaquinho,
> E que sabe um sorrisinho
> Com um jeito que consola,
> Um jeito de ser em bico
> Como o bico duma bola...

O olho preto luzia de tal maneira que se via mesmo que não cabia em si de contente. Como não coubesse em si mesmo e parecesse estar resolvido a aproveitar aquela ocasião para se pegar, ao mesmo tempo, a todas as particularidades daquele corpinho extraordinário, o olho preto rebentou. Fê-lo com tanta violência que encheu de nódoas o vestido claro da Lulu fresquíssima, o que foi uma pena.

Foi uma pena, mas eu assistia a todo este espetáculo lamentável, empoleirado a espreitar da bandeira da minha janela, num quarto ao pé do seu, na pensão em que morávamos, só então pude dizer-lhe como a conheci e amei.

Escorreguei pela parede. Rasguei-me todo na sanefa que tinha conservado alfinetadas as unhas de todos os gatos que já tivera a pensão desde o começo do mundo. Mostrei-lhe a perna onde estava impresso o seu nome dum jornal e só então, eu e ela, pudemos compreender ser minha a assinatura que faltava. Foi um momento duma emoção enorme.

A pensão era toda preta, cheirava a mofo e estava cheia de almofadas. Quando nos beijámos tudo ali se iluminou. Espalhou-se pela casa um perfume de terra molhada e as almofadas desfizeram-se em penas que encheram o ambiente de evanescências.

As penas eram brancas e cinzentas, verdes e cor de lacre, mais azuis do que o céu e, por vezes, dum alaranjado subtil como uma suspeita. Iam e vinham ao sabor da luz como o fumo – vapor das lágrimas dos olhos... Mas pegaram-se-me à vista e dissolveram a Lulu em bruma.

To please it even more, and show it the full extent of her affections, she began to sing this song which came harmoniously to her lips:

> Dear jumping little monkey,
> With my lips I made a pout,
> With the pout I made a ball,
> Then the ball I threw to you
> And it dances a hockey-cokey
> To the sound of my ukulele
> And it knows how to smile
> In a consoling way
> Spouting a pout
> Like the pout of a ball…

The dark eye gleaned so brightly that it was clear it couldn't contain itself for joy. Since it couldn't contain itself, and seemed determined to make the most of the opportunity to stick to every part of that extraordinary body at once, the dark eye burst. It burst so violently that it filled alluring Lulu's only light-coloured dress with stains, which was a pity.

It was a pity, but I watched the whole sorry spectacle, spying from the perch of my window, from a room nearby, in the boarding house where we lived. It was only then that I was able to tell her how I knew and loved her.

I slid down the wall. I tore myself on the pelmet which had held the claws of all the cats that had lived in the boarding house since the beginning of time, on pins. I showed her the leg where her name was printed from a newspaper, and only then were we both able to understand that the missing signature was mine. It was a moment of profound tenderness.

The boarding house was completely dark, it smelt damp and was full of cushions. When we kissed everything became illuminated. A perfume of wet earth spread through the house and the cushions dissolved into feathers that filled the atmosphere with ephemeral things.

The feathers were white and grey, green and the colour of sealing-wax, bluer than the sky and, sometimes, as orange as subtle suspicion. They came and went like smoke in the light – the steam of tears… But they stuck to my eyes and dissolved Lulu into mist.

CAPÍTULO IV

CHAPTER FOUR

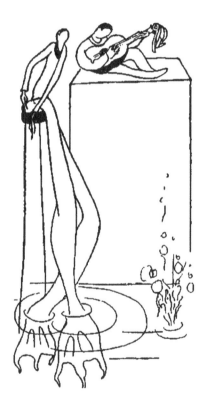

Um dia entrei num bar.

One day I went into a bar.

Assim a tive, assim a perdi como uma esperança!

Longos meses vaguei ao sabor das correntes e a sua lembrança colava-se ao meu remorso como um cheiro. Perdera a infância numa guerra, perdia agora a juventude num sobressalto. Ficava-me a vida – a coisa mais inútil de tudo o que houvera ganhado.

Fui acrobata de circo, pássaro de floresta, som de búzio, campainha de porta, ladrão de enterros, diplomata, banqueiro e cicerone. Acomodei a minha pele à cor das pedras e fui camaleão. Habituei a minha boca ao sabor das injúrias e fui prostituta. Limei as unhas ao jeito dos espinhos e fiz-me santo. Abri chagas ao longo dos membros e fui mendigo de feirantes. Enchi-me de avidez e fui prestamista como todos os hipócritas. Lavei o coração em água salgada e fui pregador de moralidades. Afligi-me de medos irremediáveis e fui herói. Atafulhei-me de culturas mortas e fui sábio. Esperei sombras nas sombras, cheio de angústia, e fui assassino. Trafiquei lágrimas roubadas, e fui comerciante. Nasci das árvores, rosado, e fui fruto apetecível. Acomodei-me, pelintra, no arredor das cidades e fui subúrbio. Conduzi homens para que morressem longe e fui general. Levaram-me em triunfo, entre archotes e flâmulas, e fizeram-me rei. Fui coveiro, serrador, águia, bússola, carneiro, violador de donzelas e menina desvirgada. Fui senhora séria, da sua casa, bicho-de-conta, camelo do deserto, satélite de estrelas, verme da terra, anjo da guarda, e apodreci, caranguejo, nos montinhos do patelo. Fui flor, rabeca, zunido do vento e água coalhada. Andei no fundo do mar e fui dos peixes sem olhos. Espalharam-me, loiro, pelas leiras, e fui milho de resteva, com pouca palha, depois do tempo. Fiz cama de maravalhas, sob os cardos, fugi ao caçador, e fui coelho do monte. Piquei os dedos das costureiras e fui agulha de ganhar o pão. Fui pinheiro de pinhão e fui pinhão de pinho bravo, caí como uma estrela na areia à minha espera. Fui rola, lagarto, cofre-forte, asa de anjinho de procissão, pendão de irmandade, esfregão, corda de enforcado, e fui enfeite de andor. Andei no marulho do mar, no ruído das oficinas de serração, nos caixotes da imundície, na mesa da anatomia, no tremor dos possessos, no choro das crianças, no rocio das manhãs, na doença das vacas, na música das romarias. Fui mentira e andei de boca em boca, cantiga e esquecia-me nos lábios, blasfémia e enrosquei-me nos santos, prece e desfiz-me nos templos, ansiedade e enterraram-me na vala comum das cidades, alegria e desfiei-me em lágrimas, afronta de rico e envergonhei-me à noite, lástima de miserável e sonhei cadafalsos. Fui verdugo e proxeneta, mártir

And so I had her, and lost her, like a lost hope!

For many months I drifted with the tides, and her memory stuck like perfume to my remorse. I had lost my childhood in a war, and now I suddenly lost my youth. My life, the most pointless thing I had gained, was all that remained.

I was an acrobat in the circus, a bird in the forest, the echo of a sea shell, a doorbell, a body-snatcher, a diplomat, a banker and a chaperone. I changed my skin to match the colour of stones and became a chameleon. I trained my mouth to slander and became a prostitute. I filed my nails to thorns and made myself a saint. Sores opened in my limbs and I became a beggar in the markets. I became full of greed, a pawnbroker, like all hypocrites. I rinsed my heart in salt water and became a moral preacher. I was assaulted by irreparable fears and became a hero. I crammed myself with dead cultures and became a sage. I waited for shadows amongst the shadows, in torment, and became a murderer. I traded in stolen tears, and became a merchant. I was born of the trees, rosy, and became a juicy fruit. I shabbily built my home in the outskirts of the city, and became suburban. I led men to die far away and became a general. They carried me in triumph, with torches, and crowned me king. I was a gravedigger, a sawyer, an eagle, a compass, a lamb, a rapist of maidens, and a deflowered young girl. I was a dutiful lady of the house, a woodlouse, a camel in the desert, a satellite of stars, an earthworm, a guardian angel, and I rotted, like a crab, on heaps of fish manure. I was a flower, a fiddle, a rustle of wind, stagnant water. I walked on the bottom of the sea and was one of the eyeless fish. They spread me, unripened, over the furrow and I became millet, with little straw. I made a bed of wonders under the thistles, I fled from the hunter and became the mountain rabbit. I pricked seamstresses' fingers and was the bread-winning needle. I was a pine tree that gave pine nuts and the pine nut of the pine tree, I fell like a star on the sand that awaited me. I was a dove, a lizard, a safe, the wing of a processional angel, a guild-banner, a mop, a hangman's rope and the ornaments of a saintly procession. I walked the bellows of the sea, to the sound of the saw mills, in the filthy bins, on the anatomy table, in the madmen's tremors, in the children's weeping, in the morning dew, in the cows' diseases, in the music of religious festivals. I was a lie that passed from mouth to mouth, a song forgotten on the lips, a blasphemy and I rubbed myself against the saints, a prayer and I dissolved myself in the temples, anxiety and they buried me in the city's common graves, joy and I burst into tears, rich men's insults and I was ashamed of myself at night, poor men's laments and I dreamt of the scaffold.

e cantador. Fiz-me pedra na montanha e ardi em fogo nos brasidos. Trouxe-a comigo, sempre, em todas as metamorfoses.

Um dia entrei num bar. Havia no bar quatrocentas colheres à roda de cada homem sentado nos bancos de pernas altas e finas como um arame sem consistência. Por baixo, no chão, era tudo água gasosa – uma espécie de géisers que brotavam de espaço a espaço, com emanações quentes de cebola e queijo.

Os homens do bar estavam todos contentes, como é costume, e riam imenso para que nenhuma dúvida fosse possível sobre a alegria com que espatuchavam os pés de palmípede na água que se ia esverdeando à medida que a lua, dependurada do teto, tomava, mais e mais, um ar veneziano.

Isto foi criando um ambiente de saturação até que rompeu uma música de guitarras que pareceu absolutamente indispensável. Todos tocavam no que tinham, e, aos homens, era-lhes sobretudo fácil fazê-lo entre as membranas dos pés. Estes, com o roçar das unhas, por causa do trémulo e com a vibração das cordas, por causa das notas mais agudas, foram tomando um ar arroxeado de coisa que já não presta.

Todos acabaram por deitá-los fora, atirando-os ali para a água que havia em volta. Era um espetáculo curioso que dava imensa fome.

Um dos pés começou, sozinho, a erguer as velas e, na corrente de ar entre a porta e a janela, circulou indefinidamente até ser como o fumo dum cigarro, às argolas, como é tão difícil de fazer. Os homens do bar quiseram, então, fazer todos argolas com o fumo dos cigarros, para mostrar também a sua habilidade. Foi um esforço enorme. Cada um fumou o mais que podia. O fumo foi tal que tudo subiu no ar e, lá em cima, não havia maneira de saber como é que se tinham os bocados do corpo já não contidos por nenhuma espécie de pressão exterior.

Uma boca começou a cantar esta canção desproporcionada:

> Ai quando na minha boca
> A tua boca colei,
> Sei que me deste outra boca
> Que à minha boca juntei.
> Agora com duas bocas
> Duas bocas beijarei.

Isto respirava, ao princípio, um arzinho pederasta que fez zunir os vidros do lustre em ressonância. Os ratos enganaram-se e roeram a lua como se fosse um queijo. Havia, evidentemente, um grande enervamento geral. Mas a canção era

I was a headsman and a pimp, a martyr and a singer. I turned myself into mountain rock and burnt in the embers. I carried her with me, always, through these metamorphoses.

One day I went into a bar. Inside, there were four hundred spoons surrounding every man seated on a high stool, with long, thin legs like wire. On the floor beneath there was nothing but fizzy water – geysers that erupted periodically, with warm emanations of onion and cheese.

The men in the bar were all happy, as is usual, and they laughed a great deal so as to make clear their joy at pressing their webbed feet on the water, that was turning green, as the moon, hanging from the ceiling, took on a more and more venetian air.

This gradually created an atmosphere of saturation, until guitar music broke out, which seemed absolutely indispensible. Everyone played the instruments they had and, for the men, it was particularly easy to do so between the membranes of their feet. These membranes, owing to the scratching of nails, the tremors and vibrations of the chords, the sharper notes, took on the purple hue of something that has gone off.

They all finally threw them away, into the surrounding water. It was a curious spectacle that made one very hungry.

One of the feet began, of its own accord, to hoist sails and, in the draught between the door and the window, it circled aimlessly until it was like rings of cigarette smoke, which are so difficult to blow. Then all the men in the bar wanted to blow smoke rings, to show how clever they were. It was a tremendous effort. Each one puffed as strongly as he could. There was so much smoke that everything floated in the air and, high above, there was no way of telling how their body parts were held together with no outside pressure.

A mouth began to sing this disproportionate song:

> Oh, when I glued your mouth
> To my mouth, I know
> You gave me another mouth
> Which I joined to mine.
> Now, with two mouths
> Two mouths will I kiss.

This initially lent proceedings a slight air of pederasty, which made the chandelier's glass tremble. The mice became confused and gnawed at the moon as if it were cheese. There was general consternation, naturally. But the song

muito mais comprida e, à medida que a ia cantando, o cantor aumentava de tal maneira que findou por quase encher o recinto todo.

Veneza acabou ali, debaixo daquela gordura inaceitável, e tudo se avermelhou como em certas madrugadas em que o céu parece amarelo e se tem muito frio.

Os homens do bar tiveram que bater com as quatrocentas colheres no cantador, até lhe desfazerem a pele completamente.

Foi uma porcaria indispensável porque já ninguém podia respirar e não sobrava espaço para coisa nenhuma. Só a canção continuava apesar de tudo:

> Quando a mãe comeu o filho
> Que acabava de parir,
> O filho, por outro trilho,
> Foi aonde havia de ir.
> Saiu do ventre a chorar,
> Voltou ao ventre a sorrir.

Era perfeitamente insuportável. Os homens do bar tiveram de atirar pela janela fora, às colheradas, a gordura que cantava aquela cantiga que ficou, e, ao fim, já não havia água nem bancos – o bar deixou-se morrer como uma paisagem ao poente.

Eu emigrei para a cidade industrial.

was much longer and the singer, as he kept singing, grew until he finally almost filled the entire area.

Venice ended there, under that unacceptable obesity, and everything took on a reddish hue like in certain dawns, when the sky looks yellow and it is very chilly.

The men in the bar had to beat the singer with the four hundred spoons, until they completely demolished his skin.

It was a necessary evil, because no one could breathe any longer, and there was no more room left whatsoever. Only the song went on, despite everything:

> When the mother ate the child
> She had just given birth to,
> The child, by another path,
> Went were he had to go.
> He left the womb in tears,
> And returned to it smiling.

It was completely unbearable. The men in the bar had to throw the mountain of grease who sang that song out of the window, by the spoonful. Finally, there was neither water nor stools – the bar let itself die, like a landscape at sunset.

I migrated to the industrial city.

CAPÍTULO V

CHAPTER FIVE

O ladrão era gordo e tinha muitas medalhas.

The thief was fat and had many medals.

No cimo da árvore mais alta do parque da cidade fabril (entre as chaminés que circundavam o largo onde o parque se perdia) havia, atado com uma fita semelhante aos laços da primeira comunhão, um molho de raparigas apetecíveis, todas nuas, expostas ao fumo e à friagem.

Em baixo, no buraco da árvore, vivia o ladrão mais conhecido da cidade. O ladrão era gordo e tinha muitas medalhas.

Porque apetecia imenso ter aquelas meninas amarradas a ele com o laço da primeira comunhão, coberto de todas as medalhas que pendurava habitualmente nos pelos do peito, o ladrão, que se chamava Ildebrando, subia às noites pelas chaminés, escorregava-lhes pelo vazio, levezinho, e ia, com imensa palha, aumentar de tal maneira o fumo das fábricas que se toldava por completo o céu.

Assim conseguia boiar no fumo (como costumava fazer no nevoeiro para roubar as casas) e ia espetar o alfinete de cada medalha no umbigo de cada menina para que, sobre aquela alvura, o brilho das medalhas, com suas fitas encarnadas, parecesse em cada ventre uma ferida.

Gozava imenso com isso e até se punha a disfarçar enquanto não conseguia (por causa da falta de peso com que ficava no meio do fumo) cair com as meninas cá em baixo, no fofo da relva.

Fazia isto sempre que lhe não era completamente impossível e, de tanto o fazer e refazer, foi-se gastando a pouco e pouco. Do muito andar gastaram-se-lhe os pés e depois as pernas que se transformaram nuns cotinhos. Do muito escorregar pelas chaminés gastou-se-lhe toda a grossura e os braços. Às medalhas também o arranhavam muito e acabou por ficar à mercê da caridade pública, ao pé do buraco da árvore, num carrinho que lhe deram as senhoras de caridade.

Estava ali no carrinho como num vaso e fazia boa figura, porque as senhoras de caridade, quando passavam por ele, tinham sempre um regador com que o regavam como se fosse chuva só num sítio. Algumas alçavam a perna e faziam--lhe chichi em cima, o que era bom para o adubo, e tinham também uma tesoura de prata para lhe cortarem os alporques.

As meninas, essas, cansadas de estarem no ar, lá em cima daquela árvore, soltaram-se do laço e puseram-se a descer pelo tronco abaixo, como se faz nos corrimões. Magoaram-se muito porque a árvore tinha uma casca cheia de asperezas, e até deixaram, pegados a essas asperezas, muitos bocados do sexo, que era o sítio por onde lhes dava mais jeito escorregar. Os bocados deixados é que ficavam lindíssimos, assim, a tremer nos casculhos mais grossos.

O ladrão que se chamava Ildebrando e tinha aprendido a habilidade de

At the top of the tallest tree in the park of the industrial city (amongst the chimneys that surrounded the square where the park was hidden) there was a bunch of attractive girls, bound by a ribbon like that worn at first communions. They were completely naked, exposed to the smoke and cold.

Below, in the hollow of the tree, lived the town's most notorious thief. The thief was fat and had many medals.

Because he really wished to have those girls tied to him with their first communion ribbon, covered with all the medals he usually hung on his chest hair, the thief, who was called Ildebrando, would climb up the chimneys at night, slide effortlessly down them through the emptiness and, with lots of straw, greatly add to the factory smoke that darkened the sky.

In this way he could float on the smoke (as he would do in the fog in order to break into houses) and stick the pin of each medal in the bellybutton of each girl so that the glean of the medals with their scarlet ribbons looked like a wound on each tummy.

He enjoyed this immensely and would even start pretending while he was unable to fall with the girls down to the soft grass below (owing to his weightlessness among the smoke).

He did so whenever it was not absolutely impossible and, in doing so over and over again, he slowly wasted away. His feet wore down from so much walking, then his legs turned into stumps. His bulk and arms disappeared from so much sliding down chimneys. The medals also scratched him, and he ended up at the mercy of public charity, by the hole in the tree, in a cart given to him by charitable ladies.

He was in his cart, looking as if he were in a flower pot, and he looked fine, because the charitable ladies who passed by always brought a watering can to water him with, as if it only rained in one spot. Some cocked their legs and peed on him, which enriched the manure, and they also carried a pair of silver scissors with which they took cuttings.

The girls, bored of being in the air, high up on the tree, freed themselves from the ribbon and began to climb down the trunk, as if they were sliding down a banister. They really hurt themselves on the knobbly bark, and left many pieces of sexual parts clinging to its rough edges, which were the most convenient to slide down. The sexual parts left behind looked beautiful, trembling on the thickest pieces of bark

The thief who was called Ildebrando, and who had learnt to sew using his

coser servindo-se dos dentes para pegar na agulha, tendo sempre a jeito muitas agulhas enfiadas que traziam as senhoras de caridade, a pretexto de sarar as meninas das feridas que lhes tinha feito aquele escorregamento, coseu-as todas, umas às outras, de tal maneira que o sangue de cada uma começou a correr indiferentemente pelas veias de todas três. Mercê desta operação a que quiseram sujeitar-se, não eram, depois, mais do que um ramo como estes que fazem das flores, atando-as com uma ráfia.

Foi nessa ocasião que rebentou a greve geral dos operários de todas as fábricas. O ladrão era de todos o que fazia mais barulho, até que lhe meteram uma faca na boca, que lhe cortou tudo, até sair pelo outro lado da cabeça.

As meninas também gritaram muito. Alçaram-nas num florete enorme com a intenção de servirem como bandeira mas, como o florete fosse muito fino, não conseguiram ficar lá em cima, tendo a lâmina aberto através delas um buraco muito certinho.

Foram consideradas monumento nacional e, à noite, os operários que já não estavam em greve iam ver, através dos corpos das meninas assentes num pedestal, o fio de luar que cabia exatamente no sítio do florete.

Eu era como os outros um operário sem nome. As penas de amor que me levaram àquela borga inqualificável do bar, depois de mais de setenta metamorfoses, acuminaram-se numa saudade dolorosíssima quando chegou a minha vez, passado o motim, de ver o luar daquela maneira. Um desejo infinito da terra encheu-me as gengivas duma adstringência desagradável. A cidade não tinha nome. Na cidade, morto o ladrão que se chamava Ildebrando, nada tinha nome. Na cidade só apontando com o dedo se sabia ser deste ou daquele que se tratava, e nunca era de mim. Na cidade, a coisa mais difícil era apontar alguém com o dedo.

Lembraram-me os pauis onde cresce o vime e as ervas mais verdes; as pedras do mar, sem medo; aquela cantiga, tão gemida, do eixo dos carros de bois; o sol entre os pinheiros, à tarde, a carcomê-los de vermelho; as mil variantes de tom do verde das leiras do milho; as velhas à porta e o gemido das moças, por detrás dos feixes da gravanha, no monte; as casas que vieram um dia pousar, em bando, e ali ficaram... Lembraram-me as pessoas : a Maria, o Joaquim, a tia Rita; as vacas: a Pisca, a Galega, a Turina; os lugares: Fontelas, Cruzeiro... Era forçoso voltar!

teeth to hold the needle, kept the many needles the charitable ladies brought him to hand. On the pretext of healing the wounds caused by the girls' sliding, he sewed them one to the other, so that the blood of each girl began to flow through the veins of all three. As a result of this operation to which they submitted themselves, they became no more than a bouquet of flowers, bound with raffia.

It was then that there was a general strike by the workers in all the factories. The thief made more noise than anyone else, until they put a knife in his mouth, which cut him right across and came out the other side of his head.

The girls, too, shouted a great deal. They were hoisted on an enormous foil so that they might serve as a flag, but the foil was very thin and they did not remain aloft, for the blade had opened a precise incision right through them.

They were declared a national monument and at night the workers, no longer striking, would go to watch the sliver of moonlight that fit through the hole in the foil, through the bodies of the girls on a pedestal.

I, like the others, was a nameless worker. The sorrows of love, which led me to the unqualified excess of the bar, after over seventy metamorphoses, finally led to an incredibly painful nostalgia when it was my turn, once the riot was over, to see the moonlight like that. My gums were filled with an unpleasantly acidic, infinite desire for earth. The city had no name. In the city, once the thief who was called Ildebrando was dead, nothing had a name. In the city one could only know who was referred to by pointing one's finger, and I was never referred to. In the city, the most difficult thing was to point one's finger at someone.

I thought of the swamps where the wattle and the greenest weeds grow; the fearless sea stones; the wailing songs of the axles of ox carts; the sun amongst the pine trees, in the afternoon, bathing them in crimson; the thousand different shades of green of corn fields; the old women at the door and the wailing of young girls, behind the sheaves of brushwood on the hillside; the houses that one day came to rest, all at once, and there remained... I thought of people: Maria, Joaquim, aunt Rita; of cows: Pisca, Galega, Turina; of places: Fontelas, Cruzeiro... I must return!

CAPÍTULO VI

CHAPTER SIX

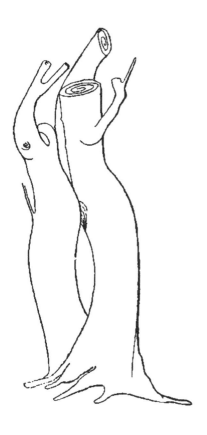

Cada árvore tem lá a sua mania.

Each tree has its own eccentricity.

Quando se volta à casa paterna tem-se sempre no coração um sabor de filho pródigo. Eu não tinha casa paterna, que ma levara a inundação, mas cheguei comprometido como se realmente houvesse pecado e não tivesse importância depois do arrependimento. Ninguém me conhecia. Trouxera das aventuras um tal aspeto de lugar-comum que não seria possível distinguir-me ninguém. Não cheguei, apesar disso, à vila. Fiquei numa falda do monte pelos arredores de Cristêlo, donde se vê o mar e a Ínsua, que tem um castelo rodeado de espuma.

Lembrei-me, então, que um dia sonhara fazer daquele castelo um refúgio de todos os poetas do mundo. Cada um faria os seus poemas e bombardeavam-se com eles, por meio dos canhões de bronze que lá estão, os navios que passassem... Talvez algum fosse de guerra e respondesse com tiros a sério! Ao fim acabava-se a poesia da terra e já se podia respirar. Até lá, devia ser ótima aquela loucura de fazer poemas só para os atirar aos navios!

Não era com esse intento que voltara, no entanto. Vinha à procura de um lugar que me contagiasse de infância. Fiz de novo a minha casa entre as árvores conhecidas. Umas estavam como as deixara. Cada árvore tem lá a sua mania. A outra mutilaram-na – podaram-na como se cada ramo tivesse de reproduzir um pescoço guilhotinado, e ela ri-se. Via-a, na véspera, chicanar do lado do paul. Ao fim estava zangada. Quando a noite se fechou como uma cortina, tinha todo o ar de quem ia pegar nas muletas e dar um passeio. Creio que foi verdade. De manhã, no dia seguinte, a soleira da minha porta estava cheia de sangue.

Na aldeia as coisas não mudam muito. Os homens lavram e fornicam, as mulheres colhem e parem, as árvores assistem. Mas, se os homens são poucos (que os levam os brasis da França e de Lisboa) as mulheres, de enormes, parece que fazem tudo.

A minha casa, fi-la pequena e com um jeito de esgar. Não a fiz a cantar como se fazem as outras casas e ela vingou-se. Quando a acabei o céu estava cheio de estrelas. Fui passear só. A noite parecia que se deixava atravessar sem resistência. Não era verdade. Na clareira do pinhal havia um dilúvio de luar. Caíam luzes doiradas e pequeninas, depois, riscando a negridão. Para fugir à saraivada de estrelas tive que acompanhar com o corpo a dança dos pinheiros, até me doerem os rins. O céu, apesar disso, tombou-me em cima como um manto furado, voltei ridículo, por entre as árvores, trazendo a noite atrás. Quando cheguei a casa, porque era preciso despir aquilo tudo, tive um frio como de inverno. Foi quase impossível adormecer.

Para entreter a insónia escrevi esta carta que me fazia falta:

When one returns to the family home one always feels, in one's heart, like the prodigal son. I had no family home, since it was carried away by the flood, but I arrived sheepishly, as if my sins were no longer relevant after my remorse. I knew no one. My adventures had made me so commonplace that it would be impossible for anyone to recognise me. Despite this, I did not return to the town. I remained in a fold of the hillside outside Cristelo, from where one can see the sea and Insua, with its castle surrounded by foam.

I then remembered that one day I had dreamt of making that castle a refuge for all the world's poets. Each poet would write his poems and throw them like bombs, by means of the bronze cannons, to passing ships... Perhaps one would be a battleship and would respond with real gunfire! Finally the world's poetry would be exhausted and one would be able to breathe again. Until that time, the madness of writing poems only to launch them at ships must be wonderful!

I had not returned with this purpose, however. I had come searching for a place to imbue me with childhood. I again built my home amongst the familiar trees. Some were as I had left them. Each tree has its own eccentricity. One of them had been mutilated – pruned as if each branch must represent a guillotined neck, and the tree had to laugh. The previous day I had seen it giggling by the swamp. It ended up getting angry. When night descended like a curtain, it looked as though it were about to take up its crutches and go for a stroll. I believe this actually happened. The following morning, the threshold of my door was covered in blood.

Things don't change much in the village. The men plough and fornicate, the women reap and give birth, the trees watch on. But if the men are few (having left for the Brazils that are France and Lisbon), the women with their huge presence seem to do everything.

I built my house small and with the air of a grimace. I didn't make it sing like other houses, and it took revenge. When I finished building it the sky was full of stars. I went for a walk, on my own. The night seemed to allow itself to be crossed without resistance. It wasn't true. In the clearing of the pine forest there was a moonlit deluge. Small golden lights then fell, scratching the darkness. To escape the volley of stars, I had to accompany the dance of the pine trees with my body until my kidneys ached. Despite this, the sky fell upon me like a shredded cloak. Ridiculous, I walked back through the trees, bringing the night with me. When I got home I had to undress it, so I was cold like in winter. I found it almost impossible to fall asleep.

To entertain my insomnia I wrote this letter, which I needed to:

«Meu amor:
Já não sei como hei de meter o ódio na minha cama! Encheram-ma de bispos e
de prédios de rendimento. Formiga lá uma canalha de todas as cores, pululante
de pessoas de família, e tem dentro tudo o que não era preciso e me deram já
feito e pronto para usar: cómodas de barriga, moralidades, poentes e tabus.
    Além disto forraram-ma toda de paisagens e, como a cada movimento se vê
uma diferente, a cada movimento toda aquela cambada começa a gritar:

– Esta paisagem é nossa!
– Que linda esta paisagem!
– Viva o Administrador do Concelho!

Foi assim que eu comecei a ter menos lugar na minha cama e a cultivar cá fora o
ódio como um brinquedo de corda. Primeiro foi para brincar e para me distrair,
agora é como quem cultiva trigo – suo todo o ano por causa do ódio e quem
ganha com isso é o intermediário... mas isso faz parte duma série de questões
sociais que não cabem numa carta de amor.
    O ódio é tão bonito! Não tem bispos nem prédios de inquilinos e gosta
imenso de espreguiçar-se ao sol.
    Sabes? E é saudável o ódio! Faz feridas em vez de ter feridas e quando gosta
duma coisa é logo para a matar. Como deve ser bom matar tudo aquilo de
que se gosta, de forma a ficar livre cá no mundo, só a contas com os nossos
inimigos!
    Escrevo-te ainda, mas esta deve ser a minha última carta. Tenho estado
doente. Doente e com dores. A doença é um ato de cobardia. Escrevo-te esta
carta como uma confissão...
    Fazia-me imenso mal o corpo todo antes de vir para aqui, para o ar, ouvir
o barulho das ondas e escrever-te, enquanto o sol me aquece as costas. Agora
parece que estou melhor porque to disse. Estou melhor com certeza. Até já
soube espreguiçar-me como o ódio!
    O mal tem, de resto, pouca importância. Provém apenas de ter inchado com
a ambição e de já não caber, à vontade, na minha cama, onde puseram aquilo
tudo que te contei. Se adoeci foi porque me aconteceu uma coisa extraordinária
na última noite em que não dormi.
    Com um pé apoiado em cada lado do meu corpo, estava um corvo preto
enorme, que marcava os minutos a balançar-se, ao compasso dos testículos.
Naquela noite houve trezentas e sessenta e cinco horas, cada uma com trezentos
e sessenta e cinco minutos, o que faz trezentas e sessenta e cinco vezes trezentas

'My darling,
I no longer know how to fit my hatred in this bed! They filled it with bishops
and rental buildings. A scoundrel of every colour worms through it, teeming
with family members, and it contains everything that is pointless, given to me
ready-made and ready-to-use: chests of drawers, values, sunsets and taboos.

Furthermore, it was upholstered with landscapes and, since with every
movement I see a different one, at every movement the rabble starts to scream:

"That's my landscape!"
"How beautiful this landscape is!"
"Long live the Mayor!"

I thus began to have less space in my bed and started to cultivate hatred outside
it, like a clockwork toy. First to play with and distract myself, now like someone
who grows wheat – I sweat all year round from hatred, and the middle man is
the only one who profits from this... but this belongs to a series of social issues
that have no place in a love letter.

Hatred is so beautiful! It has no bishops or rental buildings and it loves to
stretch out in the sun.

Did you know that hatred is healthy? It inflicts wounds instead of suffering
them and when it likes something it wants to kill it. How nice it must be to kill
everything one likes, so as to be free in the world, with only one's enemies for
company!

I'm still writing to you, but this may be my final letter. I've been ill. Ill and
in pain. Illness is an act of cowardice. I write you this letter as a confession...

My whole body hurt before I came here, into the air, to listen to the sound
of the waves and to write to you, the sun warming my back. Now I feel better
for having told you this. I am definitely better. I even used to know how to
stretch, like hatred!

The harm is, in any case, of little consequence. It is merely the result of
my having swollen with ambition and now no longer fitting comfortably in
my bed, where they placed everything I told you. If I fell ill it was because
something extraordinary happened to me on the last night I couldn't sleep.

An enormous black crow stood with a foot on either side of my body,
counting the minutes by balancing back and forth to the beat of his testicles.
That night had three hundred and sixty five hours, each with three hundred
and sixty five minutes, which adds up to three hundred and sixty five times
three hundred and sixty five times that I heard the crow's testicles rattling above

e sessenta e cinco que eu ouvi chocalhar os testículos do corvo que estava em cima da minha cama. Isto para os minutos, que as horas marcava-as ele lá cm cima, a rir no bico, com um barulho de água na pia.

Tudo por cima da minha cabeça e durou toda a noite! De manhã tinha febre.

Preciso meter o ódio na minha cama a ver se varre aquilo tudo, se mata o corvo, no caso de ele voltar a aparecer. Mas o ódio ainda não está capaz. Só tem acessos como os bonecos de corda... e ainda precisa de corda!

Tenho-o aqui, comigo, ao sol, a ver se cresce, enquanto te escrevo esta carta. O sol bate-me nas costas de tal maneira que já não sei como consigo ainda escrevê-la. Nem sei mesmo como ta hei de mandar, pois, do consolo da terra, os pés já me criaram raízes e, como as árvores, dentro de pouco já não preciso de mais que de algum estrume e de água.

Foi-me engrossando a pele e, agora, creio que já está como o cascabulho das árvores. Não é má esta sensação, embora se perca o tato mas, com o zunido do vento, no inverno, e a solidão do horizonte, deve ser triste como roupa amachucada...

Acabo, meu amor. Está a nascer-me das costas uma galha e o peso torce-me os rins.

Vê se vens, de vez em quando, dormir a sesta à minha sombra. Deixa passar uns tempos. Vem lá para a primavera. Talvez eu esteja em flor... »

my bed. This was to count the minutes, for he sounded the hours high above me, the laughter in his beak sounding like water hitting a sink.

All this was going on above my head and it went on the whole night! In the morning I had a temperature.

I need to put my hatred in my bed to see if it sweeps everything away, if it kills the crow, should he reappear. But the hatred is not yet able to do so. It only flares up sporadically, like a clockwork toy... and furthermore it needs to be wound up!

I have it here with me, in the sun, while I'm writing you this letter, to see if it will grow. The sun beats down on my back so powerfully that I don't know how I'm able to carry on writing it. Nor do I know how to send it to you because, due to the comforting earth, my feet have grown roots already and soon I will need nothing more than manure and water, like trees.

My skin has grown coarser and now I believe it is like the bark of a tree. The feeling's not unpleasant, even though I've lost my sense of touch, but with the wind howling in winter, and the loneliness of the horizon, it must be as sad as rumpled clothes...

I have come to an end, my love. A tree trunk is growing out of my back and its weight is crushing my kidneys.

Please come, once in a while, to take a nap in my shade. But not yet. Come in the spring. I may be in bloom...'

CAPÍTULO VII

CHAPTER SEVEN

Pendia-lhe do bico uma pasta de sangue.

A trickle of blood hung from its beak.

Era evidentemente mentira tudo aquilo que eu contara na minha carta de amor, ou melhor: era tão verdade que ainda não tinha acontecido. O que eu sentia podia resumir-se em necessidade do céu. O amor criara raízes, é certo mas, porque se tornara sólido e resistente, já não era capaz de moldar-se a toda a espécie de afrontas que caíam permanentemente sobre o meu corpo, fazendo-lhe a indispensável carapaça interior. Daí a constante nostalgia. Daí este querer arranhar os astros e este encolher sempre das unhas por causa do guincho insuportável. Era do céu. Era de Deus que eu precisava!

Subi então à Serra d'Arga, a mais alta destes sítios. Comecei por encontrar o caminho das cabras, entre os pinheiros, no escorregadio da gravanha não apanhada. Depois só havia cardos e terra seca. Encontrei-me ao fim entre pedregulhos e nuvens.

Era necessário que assim acontecesse. Dos primeiros caminhos pautaram-se--me os pés de cortes em comprimento. Os cardos rasgaram-me os membros, a pele do peito e a terra infetou-me as feridas. Quando cheguei ao alto, as nuvens abafaram, como algodão, os meus gritos entre pedregulhos.

Eu não sabia o que procurava mas sabia que o havia de encontrar. Por isso a alegria das minhas chagas. Por isso o gosto amargo da sufocação.

Por detrás da serra que está por detrás da serra que está por detrás da serra que está por detrás da serra que está por detrás da serra que eu tinha primeiro subido, encontrei finalmente um templo.

As colunatas do templo, enchendo-o como se fossem palmeiras num palmeiral, cortavam sempre a luz de uma sombra por cada uma.

A luz não se sabia de onde vinha. Enchia o emaranhado da catedral de uma espécie de luar leitoso. Lá ao fundo, no sítio do altar, estava evidentemente, um grande *écran* de cinema. No *écran*, os personagens eram de carne e osso. Entre eles, e a destacar-se mais nitidamente, ficava à vista, permanentemente, uma mulher tão loira como é difícil imaginar-se.

A mulher passeava sempre no *écran*, dum lado para o outro, sem que se pudesse saber exatamente o que teria com todo o romance da fita, onde havia cataratas de água caindo permanentemente.

Entre as colunas voavam pássaros cantores. Muitos pássaros voando de capitel para capitel, deixando cair no ar, como se fosse de propósito, uma espécie de chuvinha de penas que descia devagar e atapetava depois o chão de pedra, sobre o qual se andava sem barulho.

De resto, só quebrava o silêncio o cantar dos pássaros permanente, variado e múltiplo, à altura dos capitéis.

Everything I wrote in my love letter was, of course, a lie, or rather, it was so true that it hadn't yet happened. My feelings could be summed up as a need for heaven. Love had created roots, it was true, but because it had become solid and resistant, it was no longer able to mould itself to the various shocks that constantly befell my body, eating me up inside. Hence my constant nostalgia. Hence this desire to scratch the stars and this shrinking of my fingernails, due to unbearable screeching. It was heaven, it was God I needed!

So I climbed Mount Arga, the tallest hill in those parts. I began by finding the goat track among the pine trees, which was slippery with fallen pine needles. Then there were only thistles and dry earth. Finally I found myself among the stones and clouds.

It had to happen like this. The first tracks cut my feet lengthways. The thistles tore at my limbs, the skin of my chest, and the earth infected my wounds. When I reached the top, the clouds muffled my screams among the rocks, like cotton wool.

I didn't know what I was searching for, but I knew I would find it. Hence my joy at my wounds. Hence my bitter satisfaction at suffocating.

Behind the hill behind the hill behind the hill behind the hill behind the first hill I had climbed, I finally found a temple.

The temple's colonnades, filling it like palm trees in a palm grove, cut the light into shadows, one for each pillar.

One could not discern the source of the light. It filled the cathedral's tangled architecture with a sort of milky moonlight. At the back, where the altar should be, was, of course, a large movie screen. The characters on the screen were of flesh and blood. Among them, standing out most clearly, always on screen, was an unfathomably blonde woman.

The woman paced the screen from side to side, without one knowing exactly what she had to do with the movie's story, in which waterfalls flowed constantly.

Songbirds flew between the columns. Many birds flying from pillar to pillar, letting feathers drop, as if on purpose, as a sort of feathered rain which descended slowly and carpeted the stone floor, on which one could walk noiselessly.

Beyond this, the silence was broken only by the continual birdsong, varied and multiple, at the height of the pillars.

Como as penas, o cantar dos pássaros chegava macio cá a baixo.
O templo era enorme. Ao meio, no lugar da nave, havia uma clareira de colunas. Nessa clareira não havia chão. Rolava-lhe no sítio um enorme mapa-múndi, autêntico, com água e continentes, todo coberto de ar.
O ar do mapa-múndi, ao deslocar-se, enchia, mais ainda, de silêncio a catedral.
Tinha ela os muros negros do lado de dentro, negros e de veludo, a encherem-se de reflexos em tremulina. Lá no fundo, entre as últimas quatro colunas, amontoavam-se caixotes. Um deles era muito maior do que os outros e de aspeto confortável.
Por dentro era assim:
Cobria-lhe o lado que fazia de parede de trás aquele quadro de Mantegna que tem um Cristo morto na estranhíssima postura que se conhece. Os pés enchem todo o primeiro plano e, depois, tudo se estreita, cabendo em pouquíssimo espaço, por causa da deformação da perspetiva, o corpo todo até à cabeça, quase no intervalo dos pés.
Havia ainda, no caixote, uma outra caixa encostada ao quadro, com duas almofadas que pareciam duma macieza extraordinária. A cada um dos cantos, em frente desta caixa, um cavalete com uma tela.
Na caixa viviam dois irmãos gémeos e iguais, ambos pintores e pederastas, quase ruivos de loiros, sempre a sorrirem-se e a sorrir.
Os dois irmãos pintavam nas duas telas que estavam nos dois cavaletes. Os dois quadros eram iguais. A única diferença entre eles estava apenas na disposição dos motivos. O que um pintava do lado direito pintava o outro do lado esquerdo e isto era assim de maneira que fizesse sempre um rigoroso *pendant*. Tal já tinha acontecido com todos os quadros que tinham pintado os dois irmãos gémeos, loiríssimos e pederastas.
A mulher loira do *écran* via-se bem da caixa dos irmãos. Eles viam-na bem, e cada vez que disso se lembravam sorriam ainda mais.
Em certa ocasião, um dos irmãos levantou-se e foi lamber a palma dos pés do quadro de Mantegna. O outro irmão também poisou os pincéis, tirou, muito devagar, uma faca que tinha debaixo da caixa onde estavam as almofadas, e matou cuidadosamente a mulher loira que tinha saído do *écran* e estava a nadar na água do mapa-múndi.
Nenhuma das feridas da mulher deitou sangue verdadeiro. Saía-lhe luar pelas feridas, e conservava um sorriso igual ao dos irmãos.
Então, enquanto um deles lhe pintava no ventre um quadro que devia de ser

The birdsong dropped softly to the floor, like the feathers.

The temple was enormous. In the centre, there was a gap in the columns where the nave should have been. This clearing had no floor. It contained a huge, rolling globe, authentic, with water and continents, covered with air.

The globe's air, as it moved, filled the cathedral with yet more silence.

The temple had black, velvet walls inside, full of quivering reflections. At the back, between the last four columns, boxes were piled up. One was much larger than the others and looked comfortable.

Inside the box was this:

The side that served as a back wall was covered by that painting by Mantegna of a dead Christ in that curious position we are all familiar with. The feet fill the entire foreground and then the body tapers back until, owing to deformed perspective, the whole body up to the head is almost contained in the space between the two feet.

Inside the box was another box, next to the painting, with two cushions that looked extraordinarily soft. In front of this box, an easel with a canvas on it was at each corner.

Two identical twin brothers, both painters and pederasts, lived in the box, always giggling at one another and smiling, so blond they were almost ginger.

The two brothers painted on the two canvasses upon the two easels. The two paintings were identical. The only difference between them was the arrangement of the composition. What one painted on the right hand side, the other painted on the left hand side, so that the paintings were perfectly matched. This had been the case with all of the paintings by the extremely blond, pederast twins.

The blonde woman on the screen could be seen from the brothers' box. They saw her clearly, and whenever they remembered the fact they smiled even more broadly.

On one occasion, one of the brothers stood up and went to lick the soles of the feet in Mantegna's painting. The other brother also set down his brushes, removed, very slowly, a knife he kept under the box with the cushions, and meticulously killed the blonde woman who had left the screen to swim in the waters of the globe.

None of her wounds shed real blood. Moonlight issued from them, and she kept smiling, as did the two brothers.

Then, while one of them painted a picture on her belly that must have been

o centro dos outros dois que estavam nos cavaletes, o que a tinha assassinado começou a comê-la pela boca.

Comeu exatamente metade. A outra metade, comeu-a, depois, o outro irmão. Os quadros desvaneceram-se, por inúteis.

No *écran* apareceu a lua, tal e qual. Os pássaros, apressados, voltaram aos capitéis. Todo o templo se desfolhou em folhas amarelas, como se fosse outono, caídas do alto das colunas. Os irmãos deitaram-se juntos e silenciosos. Floria-lhes na boca um sorriso ainda maior.

Sobre a lua do *écran*, um pássaro, só, cantava, desvairado, um assobio sem limites. Pendia-lhe do bico uma pasta de sangue.

the centrepiece of the other two paintings on the easels, the brother who had murdered her started to eat her, beginning at her mouth.

He ate precisely half of her. His brother later ate the other half. The paintings faded away, being useless.

The moon appeared, lifelike, on the screen. The birds hastily returned to the pillars. The entire temple dissolved itself in yellow leaves falling from the top of the pillars, as though it were autumn. The brothers lay down together, silently. An even broader smile flowered on their lips.

Above the moon on the screen, a lone bird deliriously sang an endless whistle. A trickle of blood hung from its beak.

CAPÍTULO VIII

CHAPTER EIGHT

Sabes? Cresceram-me os dentes da expectativa.

You know what? My teeth grew in anticipation.

O espetáculo enchera-me duma alegria enorme. Eu quase não sabia como era. Sei que me sentia eufórico e deslumbrado. Afastei montes, pedregulhos e nuvens com as mãos e voltei à minha casa, entre as árvores, capaz de todas as falsidades.

Depois de chegar e quando me arrefeceu este entusiasmo tive uma saudade como aos quinze anos. Caí numa espécie de êxtase sensível. Uma intensa necessidade lírica exigiu-me esta carta:

«Meu amor:

Tenho demorado a escrever-te, sempre nesta esperança de que não fosse mais preciso. Contava com o esquecimento, com a morte irremediável, ou que me florissem os dedos com o fim das chuvas e me bastasse o tilintar das flores, como campainhas, a cada assomo do vento.

Afinal ainda preciso disto. É como quem arranca a crosta duma ferida. Dói, repugna imenso, mas é indispensável estar ali a escarrapitar até ao sangue...

Sabes? Cresceram-me os dentes da expectativa. Creio que foi com a posição – os cotovelos fincados no osso dos joelhos e os punhos a aguentarem sempre, pelo queixo, o peso enorme da cabeça. Fosse do que fosse, cresceram. Os de baixo subiram tão alto que andam lá em cima a confundir-se na lua. Os de cima enterraram-se na erva e vão descendo. Sinto-lhes nas pontas um frio de fundo de mar, do outro lado da Terra. Escrevo-te, assim, por detrás de grades, como uma freira. Passeiam-me aranhas sobre o dorso nu e até correm, ajeitando as patinhas frias à escada incómoda da espinha. Tinha a certeza de me excitar se não fossem a atitude e a grade dos dentes que incomodam.

De resto, não é para contar estas ninharias que te estou escrevendo esta carta. Quando vieres, se vieres e ainda for preciso, fazes casa do côncavo do meu ventre, e ajeitamo-nos, dessa forma, melhor na paisagem.

Quem me dera ser a casa onde tu mores! Crestar os pelos ao calor do lume que acendas! Sentir vibrar a pele ao eco das cantigas com que acordes! Deixar que me suguem as trepadeiras que me plantes à roda, onde se escondam os lagartos!...

Mas, por quem és, não temas o lirismo desta declaração. Por cima, a minha respiração será como um refresco, e há de o luar descer-me pelos dentes para inundar-te toda. Vestida de luar, a tua nudez deve ainda ser mais excitante que as aranhas.

Comecei a escrever para te contar uma aventura. Tenho, como de todas, a impressão que foi a única da minha vida. Era de noite e perdi demasiadamente

The spectacle had filled me with great joy. I hardly knew what had happened. I only know I felt euphoric and dazzled. I pushed aside hills, rocks and clouds with my hands, and went back home between the trees, capable of every kind of dishonesty.

Once home and when my enthusiasm cooled, I felt as nostalgic as when I was fifteen. I fell into a kind of sensorial ecstasy. An intense need for poetry made me write this letter:

'My darling,

I haven't written to you in a while, always hoping it would no longer be necessary. I was counting on forgetting, on inevitable death, or on my fingers flowering after the end of the rainy season and my only needing to tinkle them, like bells, at each breath of the wind.

But I still need this. It's like picking the scab off a wound. It hurts, it's revolting, but I need to keep digging until I draw blood...

You know what? My teeth grew in anticipation. I believe it was because of my position – my elbows resting firmly on my kneecaps and my wrists endlessly supporting the huge bulk of my head on my chin. Whatever the reason, they grew. The bottom ones grew so tall that they are up there now, being mistaken for the moon. The top ones burrowed in the weeds and are still descending. I can feel the coldness at the bottom of the sea on the other side of the earth on their tips. I write to you from behind bars, like a nun. Spiders crawl over my bare chest and they even run, beating their little cold feet against the uncomfortable staircase of my spine. I am sure I should become aroused were it not for my position and the discomfort of the bars which are my teeth.

However, it isn't to tell these trifles that I am writing. When you come, if you come and it's still necessary, make the hollow of my tummy your home, so that we can better blend into the landscape.

I want to be the house where you live! To singe my hairs by the warmth of the fire you light! To feel my skin vibrate to the echo of the songs you wake up to! To let the creepers you plant around me, where lizards hide, suck me dry!...

But, I beg you, please don't fear the poetic nature of this declaration. Above, my breath will be refreshing, and the moonlight will descend through my teeth to bathe you. Dressed in moonlight, your nakedness must be even more alluring than the spiders.

I began writing to tell you about an adventure. I have the feeling it was the only one in my life, which is how I feel about every adventure. It was night, but

a noção do tempo para te dizer há quanto tempo foi. Sei que me parecia no México, onde nunca estive, por causa dos catos e do sol.

Ela apareceu-me vestida de branco e linda a oferecer-se-me. Mexi-lhe nos olhos, que era o que mais brilhava, mas caíram no chão e quebraram-se como duas capas de vidro. Então foi o delírio. Colámos as bocas num beijo cheio de pânico e estivemos assim até ao cansaço que não vinha.

Quando acabámos estava nua. Do buraco dos olhos saíam-lhe bichos gordos que depois inchavam desmedidamente. Pareciam sexos e, como ela, era para mim que sorriam.

Houve, por isso, uma luta tremenda. Ela queria continuar a beijar-me mas os bichos comiam-me os olhos até que me foi possível morder um, cheio duma raiva que me possuiu todo. Fiquei cheio de sangue e de medo, só, no deserto de catos. Entretanto anoitecera. Adormeci no lodo vermelho.

Passaram-se meses antes que pudesse começar a mover-me. Por fim, tinha as mãos calejadas de limos e, na garganta ressequida, o ar dos pulmões, quando passava, deixava um sarro gorduroso que era o meu único alívio, embora fosse o meu enjoo.

Na paisagem de catos, o que a minha sombra pintava era como se a terra estivesse molhada.

Vês? Agora que te contei isto tudo já o coração me bate mais regularmente. Deve vir nevoeiro. Assim seja!

Talvez se me dissolvam os ossos e esta carne amolecida tenha, enfim, uma posição confortável. Talvez que fique amarrotada mas sem vincos, como um pano de borracha, à espera do fim do mundo.»

Quando acabei de escrever o que atrás fica transcrito assinei gostosamente. Ela havia de vir! Ela havia de cair como o orvalho sobre a secura da minha língua. Havia de entornar o meu olhar por ela toda, entre as sombras, passear a sua leviandade entre os ramos, como os pássaros... Havia de vir! Havia de vir!

I have lost my sense of time too thoroughly to tell you how long ago it was. I know it seemed like Mexico, where I have never been, because of the cacti and the sun.

She appeared dressed in white, beautiful, offering herself to me. I touched her eyes, the most brilliant part of her, but they fell to the ground and shattered like glass. Then came delirium. We glued our mouths together in a panic-stricken kiss and remained like that, waiting for a weariness that never came.

When we were done, she was naked. From her empty eye sockets fat slugs crept out, that kept on swelling. They looked like sexual parts and they smiled at me, as she did.

Because of this, there was a great struggle. She wanted to carry on kissing me but the slugs ate my eyes until I managed to bite one, full of a fury that possessed me completely. I was left bloody and terrified, alone, in the desert of cacti. In the meantime, night had fallen. I slept in the red dust.

Months passed before I could move again. In the end my hands were coated with slime and, in my dry throat, the air from my lungs, when it passed, left a greasy coating that was my only relief, even though it sickened me.

In the cactus landscape, the shadow I cast made the earth look damp.

Do you see? Now that I have told you all this, my heart is beating more regularly. A fog will descend. Let it be so!

Perhaps my bones will dissolve and this softened flesh will finally find a comfortable position. Perhaps I will be wrinkled but uncreased, like a rubber cloth, waiting for the world to end.'

When I finished writing the above, I signed the letter with a flourish. She would come! She would fall like dew on my dry tongue. I would spill my gaze over her whole body, amongst the shadows, promenade her frivolity among the branches, like birds... She would come! She would come!

CAPÍTULO IX

CHAPTER NINE

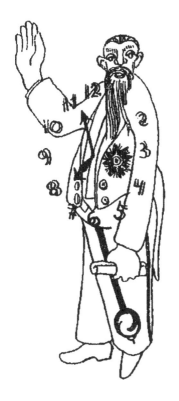

...que lhe nasceram ponteiros na barriga.

...clock hands grew on his tummy.

Na cidade, a carta foi recebida como um pedido de casamento.

Tinha-me esquecido de contar, ao longo desta história, que a Lulu era de boa família, continuava solteira e, por este tempo, já voltara a casa, perdida a esperança de se casar.

Resolveu-se então uma festa comemorativa e houve para isso convidadas e convidados. Tudo o que se passou naquela festa foi cheio de circunspeção. O pai de família deixou crescer, de propósito, uma barba para a circunstância. A mãe, de tão nervosa, virou em líquido e foi preciso arranjar uma bexiga para envolvê-la, de forma a não se perder pelas frinchas do soalho. A esse invólucro deu um artista de renome certos retoques, de forma a ficar muito parecido. Conseguiu-o tão completamente que, em vista do sucesso, assinou.

Quando chegaram os convivas tudo foram elogios à habilidade do escultor. O dono da casa estava imensamente satisfeito. Mandou toda a gente sentar-se à mesa. Pegou depois na mulher e quis levar a gentileza e amabilidade até ao ponto de servi-la como aperitivo. Ninguém aceitou. Os convidados o que tinham era fome. No entanto não pôde deixar de ser aquele discurso do velho amigo que chamou a atenção da assistência para todas as virtudes e para a seriedade moral que representava a barba tão honestamente trazida pelo dono da casa.

Enquanto o velho amigo ia fazendo o seu discurso, o homenageado ia fazendo gestos de modesto assentimento e, neste mister, batia com a cabeça tão regularmente de um lado para outro que lhe nasceram ponteiros na barriga. Foi bom porque assim toda a gente pôde saber que o discurso, fora o introito, tinha durado exatamente dez anos.

Quando acabou, os convidados estavam andrajosos e magríssimos. Foi um desespero como é fácil de calcular e sobreveio uma espécie de sublevação. Cada um se lançou sobre o que tinha mais à mão, e comeram finalmente tudo.

Era pouco. Um dos convidados mais pequenos, que era magro e tinha um queixo muito aguçado, começou a depenicar nos botões do dono da casa, em ar de brincadeira. Fazia um ruído desagradável mas ninguém lhe ligou importância de maior. Ninguém nem o próprio dono da casa podia importar-se com coisa de tão pouca monta, pois estava todo D. João V, com torneados, e quanto mais estragado mais útil seria para vender num leilão.

Deste modo tudo acabou muito bem como era de esperar. As velhas e os ossos foram dados aos cães e a gente mais moça divertia-se numa espécie de jogo a dois, que consistia em ir-se comendo cada um por seu lado, até ver quem chegava, dos pés, mais depressa ao coração do outro. O que chegava primeiro, é claro, era o que não morria logo. Mandavam-lhe vir uma padiola e depois de o passearem em triunfo, como tinha merecido, deitavam-no pela janela fora.

In the city, my letter was received as an offer of marriage.

I forgot to mention, throughout this story, that Lulu was from a good family, still single and, by this time, had returned home, having given up all hope of getting married.

A party was held to celebrate, with male and female guests invited. Everything that happened at this party was extremely circumspect. The father of the family purposefully grew a beard for the occasion. The mother, being so nervous, melted and a bladder had to be obtained to hold her, so that she wouldn't disappear between the floorboards. A famous artist gave it some finishing touches, to make it a better likeness. It was so successful that he signed the piece.

When the guests arrived they were full of praise for the sculptor's talent. The host was mightily pleased. He ordered everyone to take their places at table. He then seized his wife and was prepared to generously serve her as an aperitif. No one accepted. The guests were hungry, not thirsty. However, this did not stop the old family friend from giving a speech about the virtues and moral character represented by the beard the host had so earnestly grown.

While the old family friend gave his speech, the man being praised made modest gestures of agreement, and in doing so he moved his head from side to side so regularly that clock hands grew on his tummy. This allowed everyone to know that the speech, not counting its introduction, went on for precisely ten years.

When it was over, the guests were in tatters and extremely thin. The situation was desperate, as you can well imagine, and a sudden revolt followed. Each one threw himself on what was to hand, until they devoured everything.

It wasn't enough. One of the smaller guests, who was thin and had a very pointy chin, began to chew the host's buttons with a playful expression. He made an unpleasant sound but no one paid much attention. No one, not even the host, could care less about such a trivial matter, for his attire was all hand-turned D. João V style, and the more worn out it was, the more it would fetch at an auction.

In this way, everything ended happily, as was to be expected. The old women and the bones were fed to the dogs, and the younger guests enjoyed a couples' game, which consisted of each one eating the other, starting at the feet, to see who would reach the heart first. The winner was, obviously, the one who survived. They would send for a stretcher and carry him triumphantly, as he deserved, before throwing him out of the window.

Foi isto acontecendo até que já não havia senão um. Mandou então chamar o notário. Fez testamento daquilo que havia em casa, incluindo apólices de seguro e títulos de propriedade imobiliária, a uma instituição benemerente. Vieram os jornalistas. Tiraram muitas fotografias e puseram muitos adjetivos. O sobrevivente gostou tanto que morreu deliciado na ideia do que seriam os necrológios.

Enganou-se. Não houve necrológios nas gazetas por falta de espaço. No dia seguinte a primeira página de cada jornal vinha cheia desta notícia de sensação, em grandes parangonas:

HAVANA 5 – DIZEM DE LONDRES QUE SEGUNDO O OBSERVATÓRIO DE BOMBAIM O CÉU FICARÁ VERMELHO DURANTE TRÊS DIAS, COMO SE CHOVESSE SANGUE.

O pânico foi geral, sobretudo porque isto afinal aconteceu. Ao amanhecer, os habitantes da cidade estavam todos na rua e nas janelas, munidos de espelhos, de vidros esfumados e de bacias com água benta. Todos traziam estes utensílios por não terem coragem de olhar diretamente para o sol e, apesar disso, não serem capazes de deixar de assistir a um fenómeno anunciado com letras garrafais. Quando amanheceu e foi verdade, a confusão era geral. Houve suicídios, fugas e atropelos. Os homens fugiam, as mulheres tremiam, as crianças gritavam. Os animais, como os homens, davam mostras duma aflição irreprimível.

Ao terceiro dia, no entanto, já toda a gente estava habituada. Quando o céu voltou a ser azul, já ninguém se lembrava daquele jantar de família, e havia na terra toda um tal cansaço que parecia, a cada um, tudo mover-se ao retardador.

This went on until only one guest was left. He then called a notary. He made a will bequeathing the contents of the house, including insurance policies and real estate deeds, to a deserving charity.

The journalists arrived. They took many photographs and penned many adjectives. The survivor was so pleased that he died happy at the thought of what his obituaries would be like.

He was mistaken. The newspapers printed no obituaries, owing to a lack of space. The following day, the first page of every newspaper carried the sensational news, in large print:

'Havana, 5th: THE NEWS FROM LONDON IS THAT ACCORDING TO THE BOMBAY OBSERVATORY THE SKY WILL TURN RED FOR THREE DAYS, AS IF IT WERE RAINING BLOOD.'

There was widespread panic, especially because this in fact happened. At dawn, the city's inhabitants were all outside or at their windows, armed with mirrors, smoked glass and bowls of holy water. They carried these utensils because they didn't have the courage to look directly at the sun but, in spite of this, could not help watching the phenomenon that had been announced in such large print. When dawn broke and they saw it was true, there was general confusion. There were suicides, escapes, and trampling. The men fled, the women shook, the children screamed. The animals, like the people, showed signs of unbearable distress.

By day three, however, everyone was used to it. When the sky again turned blue, no one remembered that family dinner any longer, and the earth was filled with such weariness that everything seemed, to everyone, to move in slow motion.

CAPÍTULO X

CHAPTER TEN

a lua, certa noite, tomou um bruto pifão.

one night, the moon got terribly drunk.

Só eu ficara abandonado o tempo todo, naquele lugar do Minho que era o único que estava perto da minha pele. Arranjei cama de camarinhas junto à raiz duma árvore, à espera do meu fim. E ainda não sei se chegou...

Sei que a lua, certa noite, tomou um bruto pifão. Surgiu lá das bandas do mar inchadíssima e encarnada. Custou mesmo a despegar-se da água e deixou--a, por um tempo, cheia de malhas de sangue. Depois, andou aos tombos pelo ar e minguou. Encarrapitou-se nas nuvens, jogou com elas às escondidas e, finda a correria, caiu de cansada nas galhas dum espinheiro.

Teria ficado aí, lindíssima, se não fosse aquela moleza de queijo que a elanguescia. Assim, foi-se desfazendo numa pasta empalidecida e, devagar, entornou-se sobre mim.

Sei lá desde quando eu dormia ali, a cabeça no tufo das camarinhas, embotados os sentidos por aquele cheiro da erva fresca e da areia humedecida! Sei que com o banho da lua fiquei translúcido e molhado, bêbado e imponderável. Sei que me pegou o vento e me entremeou nos ramos das roseiras, me fez dançar na copa das árvores, rebolar nos telhados mais íngremes, descer como uma avalanche a encosta das colinas e estatelar-me nas planícies, encher-me de pólen por causa do apetite das flores. Sei que andei como uma bola de roleta no côncavo esférico do céu. Sei, finalmente que, ao bater numa estrela, me incendiei como um fogo-de-artifício.

Foi delicioso e saborosíssimo aquele crepitar de meus ossos que se haviam tornado invisíveis, aquele estalejar das bolhinhas da gordura, salpicando tudo, aquele perfume de cabelos queimados como nas estrebarias onde foi o ferrador, aquela festa de S. João na estratosfera!

Só por causa de ter batido numa estrela!

A estrela era bonita e tinha os olhos saídos como os das moscas, olhos míopes e inúteis na escuridão do céu.

Vieram-me então à memória todas as angústias do mundo – as inundações e as guerras, o medo dos fantasmas e a maldade dos homens, aquele cheiro de arroto de certas bocas que só comem o suor dos miseráveis, aquela tristeza de flor quebrada que apodreceu num monturo, aquele pst das prostitutas, aquele sorriso dos clérigos, aquele olhar para o único vestido que se rompeu, o frio e o ciúme, o tédio e a malária ao recolher das áfricas, os hospitais, as cadeias, aquele somar números abstratos toda a vida no emprego mal pago, aquele adormecer nos portais, aquele agradecer o favor indispensável, aquele ser coveiro e polícia, os leprosos, as feias, os marrecas, os generais, a morte... Ao fim fiquei como uma nuvem de cinzas.

I alone had remained abandoned all the while, in that place in Minho which was the only one close to my skin. I made myself a bed of boughs by the roots of a tree, waiting for my end to come. And I still don't know if it has come...

All I know is that, one night, the moon got terribly drunk. It rose from the confines of the sea, swollen and red. It broke away from the water with difficulty, leaving it for a while covered with threads of blood. Then it tumbled through the sky and waned. It perched on clouds, played hide and seek with them and, after the game was over, fell back, exhausted, on the branches of a hawthorn tree.

It would have rested there, beautiful, were it not for its cheese-like softness, which made it increasingly languid. It therefore started to melt into a pale paste, and slowly dripped over me.

I don't know how long I had been sleeping there, my head on a heap of boughs, my senses dulled by the smell of fresh grass and damp sand! I only know that my moon bath left me translucent and wet, drunk and weightless. I know the wind took me and cast me among the branches of rosebushes, made me dance on treetops, roll off the steepest roofs, fall like an avalanche down the hillside and crash into the plains below, filling me with pollen thanks to the flowers' appetites. I know I went about the concave sphere of the sky like a roulette ball. I know that, finally, when I collided with a star, I caught fire like a firework.

The crackle of my bones, which had become invisible, the popping of globules of fat, splattering everything, that perfume of burnt hair like the smell of a smithy, that party of S. João in the stratosphere, were delicious and supremely tasty!

And all because I collided with a star!

The star was pretty and had protruding eyes, like a fly; myopic, useless eyes in the darkness of the sky.

I then remembered all the world's sufferings – the floods and wars, the fear of ghosts and the cruelty of men, the smell of burps from certain mouths that only feed on the sweat of the penniless, the sadness of a broken flower decaying on a rubbish heap, the psst of prostitutes, the smile of clergymen, the gaze upon one's only dress, which has just torn, the coldness and jealousy, the boredom and malaria after leaving Africa, the hospitals, the prisons, the lifelong addition of abstract numbers in a poorly paid job, the falling asleep at gates, the thanking the indispensable favour, the being a gravedigger and policeman, the lepers, the ugly women, the hunchbacks, the generals, death... Finally, I was like a cloud of ashes.

Caí então de novo sobre a terra. Caí como uma chuva suave. Confundiram-
-me com o luar quando me espalhei no descampado alucinando os gatos,
pintando as casas, murchando as flores e apodrecendo o peixe... Por mim sei, no
entanto, que são humanos este gosto das surpresas e esta permanente tentação
do dilúvio. Sei que viverei eternamente embora não tenha nem intestinos nem
fígado.

I then fell again to earth. I fell like soft rain. They mistook me for moonlight when I spread over the waste land, frightening the cats, painting the houses, wilting the flowers and rotting the fish... For my part, I know, however, that this love of surprises and this permanent temptation of floods are very human. I know I will live for ever, even though I have neither entrails nor a liver.

APPENDICES

CONTO
IRRACIONAL

inédito de

António Pedro

NO cimo da árvore mais alta do parque da cidade fabril (entre as chaminés que circundavam o largo onde o parque se perdia) havia, atado com uma fita semelhante aos laços da primeira comulhão, um molho de raparigas apetecíveis, todas nuas à mercê do fumo e da friagem.

Em baixo, no buraco da árvore, vivia o ladrão mais conhecido da cidade. O ladrão era gordo e tinha muitas medalhas. Porque apetecia imenso ter aquelas meninas amarradas a ele com o laço da primeira comunhão coberto de todas as medalhas que pendurava habitualmente sôbre os pêlos do peito, o ladrão, que se chamava Ildebrando, subia ás noites pelas chaminés, escorregava-lhes pelo vasio, lèvezinho, e ia com imensa palha aumentar de tal maneira o fumo das fábricas que toldava por completo o céu.

Assim conseguia boiar no fumo (como costumava fazer no noveiro para roubar as casas) e ia espetar o alfinete de cada medalha no umbigo de cada menina para que sôbre aquela alvura o brilho das medalhas, com suas fitas encarnadas, parecesse em cada ventre uma ferida.

Gosava imenso com isso e até se punha disfarçar enquanto não conseguia (por causa da falta do pêso com que ficava no meio do fumo) cair com as meninas cá em baixo, no fôfo da relva.

Fazia isto sempre que lhe não era completamente impos-

sível, e, de tanto o fazer e refazer, foi-se gastando a pouco e pouco. Do muito andar gastaram-se-lhe os pés e depois as pernas que se transformaram nuns cotinhos. Do muito escorregar pelas chaminés gastou-se-lhe tôda a grossura e os braços. As medalhas também o arranhavam todo e ficou à mercê da caridade pública, ao pé do buraco da árvore, num carrinho que lhe deram as senhoras de caridade.

Estava ali no carrinho como um vaso e fazia boa figura porque as senhoras de caridade quando passavam por êle tinham sempre um regador com que o regavam (como se fôsse chuva só num sítio) e tinham também uma tesoura de prata para lhe cortarem os alporques.

As meninas, essas, cançadas de estarem no ar, lá em cima daquela árvore, soltaram-se do laço e puzeram-se a escorregar pelo tronco a baixo. Magoaram-se muito porque a árvore tinha uma casca cheia de asperezas e até deixaram pegados a essas asperezas muitos bocados que ficavam lindíssimos, assim a tremer nos casculhos mais grossos.

O ladrão que se chamava Ildebrando e tinha aprendido a habilidade de coser servindo-se dos dentes para pegar na agulha, tendo sempre a geito muitas agulhas enfiadas que lhe traziam as senhoras de caridade, a pretesto de lhes sarar as feridas cozeu-as tôdas umas ás outras de tal maneira que o sangue de cada uma começou a correr indiferentemente pelas veias de todas as meninas que, mercê da operação a que se tinham sugeitado, já não eram mais do que um ramo, como êste que fazem das flôres, atando-as com uma rafia.

Foi nessa ocasião que rebentou a greve geral dos operários de todas as fábricas.

O ladrão era de todos o que fazia mais barulho até que lhe meteram uma faca na boca que lhe cortou tudo até sair pelo outro lado da cabeça.

As meninas também gritaram muito. Alçaram-nas num florete enorme com a intenção de se servirem delas como bandeira mas, como o florete era muito fino elas não conseguiram ficar lá em cima, tendo a lâmina aberto, através delas, um buraco muito certinho.

Foram consideradas monumento nacional, e, às noites, os operários que já não estávam em greve iam vêr, através dos corpos das meninas, o fio de luar que cabia exactamente no sítio do florete.

Lisboa, Dezembro de 1938.

(Do livro em preparação ANTROPOFAGIA E OUTROS CONTOS)

Appendix 1

Motim: conto irracional (Strike: an irrational story) 1939

Published in *Juventude*, December 1939, p. 21. This text (but not the image) would later become part of chapter V.

Appendix 2

O Repasto imundo (The Revolting Meal) 1939

Featured in Giuseppe Ungaretti's Preface to Pedro's 1941 exhibition in São Paulo, and reproduced in *Variante*, (1942), p. 65, and in *Free Unions/Unions Libres* (1946), hors-texte 24–25.

Ultima folha de um diário de viagem

De ANTONIO PEDRO

— Ao JORGE DE LIMA —

Q UANDO eu cheguei à cidade rolou-me a cabeça que sonáculos e nos vales [...] um espetáculo maravilhoso. Os olhos foram-se-me nas arvores antigas e foram pássaros e folhas brilhando humidas nos galhos musculosos. Sabes? Havia jardins e gaiolas, peixes e laranjas por toda a parte. Nos jardins as arvores eram velhas e indiferentes. Tinham varises e às vezes sangravam dos cabelos. Via-se que cabiam historias, mas não podiam contá-las. Tinham as copas lá em cima muito altas e havia em todas um meneio de desespero que não era dificil de adivinhar.

Depois toda a população se pôs a dansar os batuque do carnaval no concavo do meu estômago. Encheram-se de vasio e poeira com uma alegria que não era de ninguem. Vestiram-se todos de poetas com folhas e setins Ao fim eram como frutos e (seu ri!), às arvores apetecia-lhe tê-los dependurados: veiu depois um poeta verdadeiro à minha casa. Semeou-me nas janelas *ladrões enforcados* e *bailarinos*. O poeta verdadeiro fez o que arvores não tiveram coragem de fazer Eu tenho a preguiça das arvores e os sonhos do poeta. Agora, na minha casa ha um cheiro de primavera. A maquina bonita do carroussel parado que é só um minho de gatos, sai da cortina com seus arames inuteis para os meus olhos cansados O calor esvasiou me a consciência e esta imaginação ador-

mecida. Quebrou no meu aquario um arranha-céus e o peixe que sobrou da hecatombe anda de andar em andar e vê-se que não sabe a côr das estrelas. Os limos das minhas mãos já são como os dos navios do fim duma viagem, e torna venenosas as ostras e caramujos. Quanto ao Cristo do Corcovado ainda mais me separa das Igrejas feito arvore de luz entre a neblina, na harmoniosa escabrosidade do monte

Ando quasi doente. A boca re cusa-se-me ao sabor das ervas que outro verde esquentou e outro socio endureceu para o pasto deste onagro filho do meu pai e da minha mãe, onde eavalgo — Quichote e Sancho, — à busca de moinhos que não ha. O sol cegou os meus olhos para outra luz que não seja esta de contornos agrestes e de sombras recortadas

Não sei que fome me tomo de alçar até ao céu as janelas do quarto que não tenho de forrar tudo de veludo e de apagar as luzes, de me arrancar os olhos e de me por a adivinhar-me nelas.

Eu sei exatamente do que se trata.

Quero saber se eu em verdade se-

rei apenas aquela arvore que se move, sem folhas e sem frutos só com flores e vestigens. Se serei aquela alga do mar que as correntes arrastam à babugem de todas as areias, e foi enfeite de embarcações, e foi brinquedo de banhista e foi cama de caranguejo e escondérijo de polvo e serviu de leito ao amor de todos os bichos do mar e ha-de ser estrume da terra quando a colherem um dia. Quero saber se em verdade serei aquele lobo que comeu o cordeiro e depois só podia pastar naquele vale verde que só havia cardos.

Sabes? Depois desta viagem só poderei fazer outra viagem. Sinto já nos ossos meu cansaço de fim de mundo e aqui este sol vai amadurecer-me a carne por completo.

Depois será lindíssimo o meu fim. Hei de procurar uma planicie sem sombras. Hei-de plantar-me no meio, enorme, como uma doença da terra. Depois escorregar-me-ão as felções até ao chão. Ficarei ai como uma mancha até às primeiras chuvas. Se vieres por esse tempo colhe num vaso alguns torrões Devem servir para fazer crescer as orquideas e os fetos.

Appendix 3

'Última folha de um diário de viagem' ('Last page of a travel diary') 1941

Published in the Brazilian newspaper *Dom Casmurro*, 26 April 1941. The press cutting can be found in Pedro Archives (E5/638).

Appendix 4
untitled 1942

Reproduced in *Panorama* (9), Junho 1942, p. 17. This drawing, most likely a study for the cover of the first edition of *Just a Story*, was displayed in the 1ª Exposição dos artistas ilustradores modernos (Lisbon, April; Porto, May; 1942) with the indication 'Ilustração para o romance "Apenas uma narrativa", de António Pedro'.

Appendix 5
Nude Woman 1945

Reproduced in *Catalogue of Modern British and Continental Drawings, Paintings and Sculpture: The Property of the late E. L. T. Mesens [26 April 1972]* (London: Sotheby, 1972). This picture was probably painted in England by Pedro and displayed in one of the exhibitions organized by the London Gallery in the 1940s. Auctioned in 1972 by Sotheby's.

When one returns to the bosom of the family one always has the feeling of being a prodigal son. I had no paternal home, for it had been carried away by a flood, but nevertheless I arrived with the same feeling as if I had really sinned and the sin was forgotten upon repentance. No one knew me. I had brought back from my adventures such a commonplace appearance that it was impossible for anyone to recognise me. In spite of this, I never went to my manor-house. I stayed at the foot of the hill on the outskirts of Cristelo, from which one can see the sea and Insua, that has a castle surrounded by foam.

I remembered then that I had once dreamed of turning that castle into a refuge for all the poets in the world. Each one would write his own poems and then use them, with the help of the bronze cannon there, to bombard any ships that might pass by . . . Perhaps one might be a warship and would reply with serious counter-fire. Finally, all the poetry on earth would be exhausted and one would be able to breathe. Until then, it should be a wonderful madness, that of writing poetry simply to fire at the ships.

It was not, however, for this purpose that I had returned. I came to search for a place which might remind me of my childhood. I once more built my house among the familiar trees. Some were as I had left them. Each tree is mad in its own way. Another had been mutilated—pollarded as if each branch must represent a guillotined neck, and looked as if it were laughing. I saw it the day before, mocking from the edge of the fen. In the end it was thoroughly annoyed. When night closed in like a curtain, the tree looked like someone about to pick up his crutches and go out for a walk. I think it must have been so, for on the morning of the following day, the threshold of my door was covered in blood.

There is little change in the village. The men sow and procreate, the women reap and give birth, and the trees look on. But if the men are few (having gone fortune hunting in France and Lisbon) the women, being so large, seem to do everything.

I built my house small, and like a grimace. I did not make it singing, as others do when they build their houses, so it took its revenge on me. When I finished it, the sky was full of stars. I went for a walk on my own. The night looked as though it would offer no resistance to anyone passing through it. But this was not the case. In one of the woodland glades there was a flood of moonlight. Little gilded lights rent the darkness as they fell. In order to escape the hailstorm I had to let my body follow the dance of the pinetrees until my back ached. Nevertheless the sky descended upon me like a torn cloak. I returned, ridiculously, through the trees, with the night dragging behind me. When I reached home, and had to remove all that, I felt as cold as winter. It was almost impossible to sleep.

To alleviate my insomnia I dealt with a letter that I had long been meaning to write:

"My darling,

I don't know how to contain my hate in this bed. It is filled with bishops and rented buildings. There swarms a rabble of all colours and it seethes with hoards of relations and contains everything useless that has been given to me, ready for use: chests of drawers, moralities, sunsets and taboos.

Apart from all this, it has been lined with landscapes and as with every movement one sees a fresh one, at every movement the whole gang start to shout : 'This landscape is ours! How beautiful this landscape is! Long live the Mayor!'

ANTONIO PEDRO
from Just a Story

So I began to have less and less room in my bed and to cultivate outside my hate, like a clockwork toy. At first this was simply as a toy to amuse me, but now it is like growing wheat—I sweat throughout twelve months of the year on behalf of the hate, and the person who reaps all the benefit is the middle-man . . . but this is one of many social questions and has no place in a love letter.

The hate is so beautiful. It has neither bishops nor tenements and it loves to stretch itself out in the sun. Do you know? This hate is salutary. It inflicts wounds instead of receiving them, and when it loves anything it prepares to kill it straight away. How nice it must be to kill everything one loves and so live freely in the world, to settle accounts with one's enemies!

Although I am writing to you now, this will probably be my last letter. I have been ill. Ill and in pain. Illness is an act of cowardice. I write this letter as a confession . . .

My body treated me very badly until I came out here into the fresh air, to hear the sound of the waves and to write to you while the sun warms my back. Now it seems that I am all the better for having told you. I am definitely better. I can even stretch myself out, like the hate.

The harm is, in any case, of little importance. It is merely the fruit of my being swollen with ambition and being no longer able to fit comfortably into my bed which is full of everything I have already mentioned. If I became ill, it was because of something that happened to me on my last sleepless night.

With a foot planted on each side of my body, was an enormous black crow, who marked the minutes by swaying in time with its testicles. That night there were 365 hours, each one with 365 minutes, which makes 365 times 365 that I heard the beating of the testicles of the crow that stood on my bed. This was for the minutes. He marked the hours above, by laughing in his bill with the sound of water in a cistern.

All this over my head and all through the night! In the morning, I was feverish.

I must put my hate into the bed and see if it will clean it all up, and kill the crow if it should happen to come back. But the hate isn't yet strong enough. It only has spurts, like a clockwork toy—and it still needs winding up.

I have it here with me, in the sun, to see if it will grow while I am writing this letter. The sun is beating down on me so strongly that I don't know how I can manage to go on writing this letter. Nor do I know how I shall send it to you since, with the comfort of the earth, my feet have grown roots and, like the trees, I shall soon need no more than a little manure and water.

"My skin has coarsened and now I think that it is like the bark of a tree. This sensation is not unpleasant, although one loses the sense of touch but, with the howling of the wind in winter, and the bare horizon, it must be as sad as rumpled clothing . . .

I have come to an end, my love. A gall-nut is growing from my shoulders and its weight is twisting my kidneys. See if you could come, sometimes, to take your siesta in my shade. But not yet. Come in the Springtime. Perhaps I will be in flower . . . "

Translated from the Portugese by D. M. EVANS.

6   The complete novel will appear in the London Gallery Editions.

Appendix 6
English translation of Chaper VI of *Just a Story*

Published in *Free Unions/Unions Libres* (London: Express Printers, 1946), p. 6. The complete translation of *Just a Story* was never published.

CHAPTER EIGHT - 3 *(they beeing)*

~~hurxt~~ herself to me.   I touched her eyes ~~-~~ (the most brilliant
part of her - but they fell to the ground and broke like two pieces
of glass.   Then came delirium.   We glued our mouths together in
a panic-stricken kiss and remained immobile, waiting for the
weariness that never came.

When we drew apart, she was naked.   From her empty
eyesockets crept fat slugs that later swelled enormously.   They
were like two phalli
~~all seemed to be female~~ and, like her, it was at me that they
smiled.

Then took place, on account of this, a fierce battle.   She
wanted to go on kissing me, but the slugs ate my eyes until I was
able to bite one, being seized by a great fury that completely
possessed me.   I was left bloody and terrified, alone with the
desert of cacti.   Meanwhile, night had fallen.   I slept in the
red dust.

Months passed before I was able to move.   In the end my
hands were coated with slime and the breath from my lungs left, in
my parched throat, a greasy coating that formed my only relief,
although it sickened me.

In that cactus filled landscape, the shadow that I cast made
the earth look damp.

You see!   Now that I have told you all this, my heart is
beating more regularly.   Surely a mist will rise.   Pray God it
may!

Perhaps my bones will dissolve and this softened flesh will
find, in the end, a comfortable position.   Perhaps I shall remain

Appendix 7

Sample of D. M. Evans' unpublished translation of *Apenas uma narrativa*,
with Pedro's handwritten revisions, Chapter VIII, page 3, undated

'(Just a Story)', E. L. T. Mesens papers, Getty Research Institute, California, box 14,
folder 5. The papers do not include the preface (see next appendix).

$E_5/417$

PREFACE - 2

~~Insanit~~ "novel"~~t~~. In Brazil, some time ago, there was a great
discussion between writers concerning what should be designated as
a "novel" and what should be termed a "story".[1] All of their
arguments were~~,~~ _{So} reasonable ~~but~~ ^{that} only one reached the point of
terminating further discussion on the subject. Some voted for the
question of length; others for content, others for the manner of
unfolding the tale. But I consider that of all theories, Mario de
Andrade's was the best: "A Novel is anything to which its author
decides to ascribe that title".

The tale which you are about to read is as simple as the
plants and grew up naturally ~~with~~ ^{like} them, although, like them, it may
have unexpected forms. It does not pretend to prove anything, but
if it did, it would be that there is a logic of nonsense just as
there is a rational logic, much more spontaneously acceptable and -
^{I know how to}
were it ~~not~~ dangerous to broach such subjects - ~~one which is~~ much
nearer to the logic of ^{the} artists ~~than other~~ ^(understood by the) (people ~~realise~~; - fête-day
potters who fashion gilt cats with red spots and human faces; story-
tellers at provincial soirées, who invent such tales as that of ~~Gxx~~
Cinderella's pumpkin coach~~,~~ ^{and} that remarkable and unknown poet who
wrote "Rico pico serenico, quem te deu tamanho bico ou de ouro ou de
prata mete aqui nesta buraca".[2]

_____

(1) The portuguese words are; Romance *novel* and *novela* (story)
(2) A children's counting rhyme, like "Each peach pear plum out
goes Tom Thumb"

Appendix 8

Sample of English translation of the Preface for *Just a Story*,
with Pedro's handwritten revisions, undated

'Just a Story: preface', Pedro Archives, Biblioteca Nacional de Portugal, Lisbon, E5/417.
Probably also translated by D. M. Evans.

Appendix 9
untitled undated

Reproduced in *Centro de Estudos do Surrealismo: cadernos*, (10), December 2011, p. 7. This watercolour is a variation of the illustration which opens Chapter I, depicting Adam. It belongs to Fundação Cupertino de Miranda (V. N. Famalicão, Portugal).

Appendix 10

Femme-oeils (Woman-eyes) undated

Reproduced in José-Augusto França, 'Estudo de uma pintura de António Pedro', *Colóquio-Artes*, December 1973, p. 18. This variation of the illustration which opens Chapter III, depicting Lulu, was subsequently further reworked in Pedro's masterpiece, *Rapto na paisagem povoada* (1946), which features a similar statue as part of the overall composition.

Appendix 11
A Ínsua (1937)

Reproduced in *António Pedro (1909–1966),* (Lisbon: Fundação Calouste Gulbenkian, 1979), p. 19.

Ínsua is a small island in the north of Portugal, alluded to in Chapter VI of *Just a Story.*

Printed and bound by CPI Group (UK) Ltd, Croydon, CR0 4YY

13/04/2025

14656597-0003